Arizona Range War

J.T. Edson

Arizona
Range War

WHEELER
PUBLISHING, INC.
ROCKLAND, MA

★ AN AMERICAN COMPANY ★

4699203

Published in Large Print by arrangement with
Dell Publishing, a division of Bantam Doubleday Dell
Publishing Group, Inc., in the United States and Canada.

Wheeler Large Print Book Series.

Set in 16 pt. Plantin.

Library of Congress Cataloging-in-Publication Data

Edson, John Thomas.
    Arizona range war / J.T. Edson.
        p. (large print) cm.(Wheeler large print book series)
    ISBN 1-56895-412-3 (softcover)
    1. Large type books. I. Title. II. Series
[PR6055.D8A89 1997]
823'.914—dc21   96-39742
                                                                CIP

For my nursemaid-cum-minder, Maggie McGhie, who always gets us from here to there and back the longest way with stops for a Coors "heavy" beer, or six, at Jeff's Pub in Tucson and the Rusty Spur at Scottsdale in passing.

Author's Note

While complete in itself, this narrative follows immediately after the events recorded in WEDGE GOES TO ARIZONA.

When supplying us with the information from which we produce our books, one of the strictest rules imposed upon us by the present-day members of what we call the "Hardin, Fog, and Blaze" clan and the "Counter" family is that we never under any circumstances disclose their true identity or their present locations. Furthermore, we are instructed to always employ enough inconsistencies with regard to periods and places in which incidents take place to ensure that neither can happen even inadvertently.

We would also point out that the names of people who appear in this volume are those supplied to us by our informants in Texas, and any resemblance with those of other persons, living or dead, is purely coincidental.

To save our old hands repetition, but for the benefit of new readers, we have given "potted biographies" of Captain Dusttine Edward Marsden "Dusty" Fog, Mark Counter, and the Ysabel Kid in the form of Appendixes.

We realize that, in our present permissive society, we could use the actual profanities employed by various people in the narrative. However, we do not concede that a spurious desire to create realism is any justification for doing so.

Since we refuse to pander to the current trendy usage of the metric system, except when referring to the caliber of certain firearms traditionally measured in millimeters—e.g., Luger 9mm—we will continue to employ miles, yards, feet, inches, pounds, and ounces when quoting distances and weights.

Lastly, and of the greatest importance, we must stress that the attitudes and speech of the characters are put down as would have been the case at the period of this narrative.

J.T. Edson
Melton Mowbray
Leics.,
England

Arizona Range War

I CHOOSE WHEN— AND *WHO*— I FIGHT!

"It's goddamned lucky for Eustace Edgar Eisteddfod, as he liked to be called, that he got killed the way he did!" Anthony Blair snarled furiously. Even after many years in the United States, he had an accent that gave evidence he had grown up in Birmingham, England. He was small, lean, and had parchmentlike sharp features that were not rendered any more likable by his buckteeth, and there was something weasel-like in his appearance and demeanor. His clothing was Eastern in style and of such sober hue that, taken with his usual expression of piety, he looked like an undertaker, even though he was occupying the best suite offered by the Spreckley Hotel in Prescott. Elsewhere throughout Arizona, the most noticeable thing about him would have been that there was no sign of his being armed in any way. However, this was no particularly noticeable omission in the capital of Arizona. "After all the money we put for setting him and those other three bastards he brought in up with the ranches in Spanish Grant County. Then, after he'd fixed it for two of them to be put under, it turned out that, unbeknown to him, they'd both made wills that left theirs to kinfolks instead of sticking to the original deal."

"He did get Hayes of the Arrow P without that having happened, though," Willis Norman pointed out in a surly New England voice. He

1

had been the one responsible for recruiting and leaving the removal of the other three ranchers in the hands of the man who claimed to be of Welsh descent, and he did not care to be reminded how badly the scheme had gone wrong. Although they were partners in a scheme by which they hoped to make a fortune apiece and gain positions of great power in Arizona, there was a great contrast in appearance between himself and the other speaker. He was close to seven inches taller than Blair and weighed nearly twice of as much. Massive of lines and porcine of face, his bulky body strained at the costly Eastern garments he had on; he, too, gave no indication of bearing armed weapons. "Anyway, it's no use crying over spilled milk. What we have to do now is see how we can bring off the takeover of that damned Spanish grant regardless of who owns what there."

Because Congress had ratified the Spanish grant for its original owner when the annexation of Arizona by the United States was completed on February 24, 1863, the vast area of land that became the county of that name remained under his control despite the envious eyes that were constantly being cast upon it by various American speculators eager to gain possession of it. His dominance had been far from despotic. In fact, he had allowed a town owned by American businessmen of various kinds to rise in the center of the area. When he died intestate and no one of his race put in claims, the government in Washington, D.C.—many members of which had never really favored the proposition of one person, especially one who retained Mexican citizenship, owning so much United States' soil—

had ruled that it would be divided into four equal portions demarcated by natural features such as hill ranges and rivers.

Hearing what was proposed through sources in the national capital before the matter was made public, Blair, Norman and their third partner, Graeme Steel—who would be joining them shortly with one of the men essential for their future arrangements in the light of the less than satisfactory developments under discussion—had seen a way to acquire the whole region. They had known any attempt to bring this about as a single corporation would be resisted strenuously and probably be to no avail, so they had sought for a man sufficiently ruthless to carry out their scheme. Having been acquainted with Eisteddfod under a different name in Washington, D.C., Norman had claimed that his knowing something of the reason for the change of identity made him perfect for their needs.

From the beginning, the alleged Welshman had carried out his duties to the complete satisfaction of his employers. He had selected the candidates for ownership of the other three ranches and made them agree to a contract drawn up by an attorney in Prescott whereby any who died let his land be shared between the survivors.

At first, despite there being no profit accruing in return for the considerable expenditure required, the arrangements went along in a manner that met with the approval of the three conspirators. Having allowed sufficient time to elapse for the quartet to become accepted as bona fide landowners, even though only

Cornelius MacLaine had had experience of the cattle business and they were dependent on their respective foremen to carry out the running of the ranches, they had instructed Eisteddfod to begin the next stage of the scheme.

With the aid of an ex-jockey called Beagle who had been barred from employment in that line for dishonesty, the "Welshman" had arranged for Douglas Loxley of the Lazy Scissors ranch to die by what appeared to be a riding accident. Too late it had been discovered that the ranch had been left in an incontestable will to a kinsman, Major Wilson Eardle, who had recently retired after a career with the United States Cavalry. To make matters worse, when a similar fate befell MacLaine, who ran the CM brand, he too had arranged for the property to go to a relative, his nephew Jethro "Stone" Hart, a Texan well-known for running a group of very competent and loyal contract trail drivers known as the Wedge. The three conspirators had decided that Hart, more experienced in all matters pertaining to the cattle business and the ways of the West, would prove much the tougher nut to crack.

It had been Eisteddfod who suggested what might be done to ensure the success of their scheme. He received the backing they required, including support of a group of young Easterners donated by some of the wealthy liberals in Washington, D.C.—who had no desire to see Arizona attain statehood unless they could gain at least some control of its legislature. The "Welshman" had set about trying to create hostility between the two new ranch owners and stir up animosity against them in Child City,

4

the seat of what was now known as Spanish Grant County. There had followed a series of failures that ended with Eisteddfod, Beagle, and the leader of the hired guns who were supplied by the conspirators dead, fortunately without any of them being able to tell what had brought them to their fate.

With so much money already invested in the scheme, despite having found that the liberals were disinclined to provide more financial aid, the conspirators had no intention of relaxing their efforts. They had reached agreement about how the desired results could be achieved, and the meeting that night in the hotel was for the purpose of obtaining the means to let the various parts of the scheme be put into effect.

Before either of the partners could continue what appeared likely to develop into another of their frequently acrimonious debates—none was willing to accept the assumption by another of the two that he was the senior—the front door of the suite was opened without the formality of a knock. Through it came the third member of their alliance and a second man they both recognized as being previously of use to them and now to be an essential factor in their scheme.

In many respects, Graeme Steel was an even less noticeable figure than his two companions. In height and build between them, everything about him—even his city-style clothing—was so ordinary in appearance that he could easily have passed unnoticed through a crowd at any level of Prescott society except where those who wore attire peculiar to their specific line of work were concerned. He had mouse-brown hair left visible by the plain gray derby hat he was carrying and a face so devoid of characteristics as to be unlikely to attract notice. Despite being equally wealthy and unscrupulous, he seemed to have nothing in common with his associates. Nevertheless, like them, he possessed a number of contacts of vital importance, and it was one of these by whom he-was accompanied.

John Nicholson looked like many other bureaucrats of his level in every government and state agency in the nation. The garments and the jewelry he sported suggested that he was not living solely upon his earnings as the senior land agent for the Territory of Arizona. About five feet seven in height, he had a thinning thatch of reddish-brown hair plastered down by a liberal application of bay rum, and his pallid and far-from-handsome features normally bore an expression of condescension created by his knowledge of the power he could wield by virtue of his position. However, his face looked more disturbed than haughty at that moment; he had no reason to be pleased by the summons he had received, though he knew he did not dare refuse.

"I've Haynes Lashricker and two more of the hired guns waiting in the bar downstairs," Steel announced in a voice devoid of accent or tone. "But I thought we'd better deal with our *friend* here first. I'm sure he's got some pressing matters demanding his attention, and we wouldn't want to keep him from her—*them*—would we?"

"W-What can I do for you, gentlemen?" Nicholson queried. His voice held none of the pompous tone that he, like many of his kind, adopted when dealing with persons he considered of no importance or potential influence.

"You've heard about what's been happening in Spanish Grant County, haven't you?" Blair asked, realizing—as did Norman, if his baleful scowl was any indication—that Steel had brought the visitor only to ensure that he alone could not be held responsible for anything that might go wrong.

"Of course," Nicholson confirmed, remembering the part he had played in the four men obtaining possession of the ranches.

"And you've heard that Mr. Eisteddfod and Mr. Hayes have left their properties to relations?" the weasel-featured conspirator went on.

"No," the land agent denied. His anxiety had been increasing since he had received the command to meet with Steel.

"Well, they did," Blair stated. "And you'll be receiving the documentary proof in a couple of days' time."

"I will?" Nicholson queried, and his worried look grew even more noticeable.

"You will," Blair confirmed. To ensure that any blame could be shared by his two partners, he continued, "We *all* can guarantee that."

"Th-Then the matter will be easy to resolve," the land agent asserted, recalling how all the necessary documentation for the transaction that had put the four ranches into the possession of their owners had been so impeccably produced that it was impossible to be proved other than genuine. "All the beneficiaries have to do is bring proof of their claims to *my* office and I can register their ownership."

"Then that's all we need to see you about for the time being," Steel said with mock gratitude. "I hope we haven't made you late for Michele."

"N-No!" the land agent answered, wondering how this man had learned about his connection with the woman who did not have the same name as his wife. "Can I go now?"

"Go ahead," Steel authorized. Then, after the land agent had taken a hurried departure, he went on, "Well, there's one we don't need to worry over. With what I have on him, there's *nothing* could make him tell what he's up to or knows about us. Call downstairs on the voice pipe, one of you, and tell them to send the three from the bar up here to us."

Scowling, Norman did as suggested.

After a short time, three men who were as unlike in appearance as the partners came into the room!

In the lead, twenty-year-old Michael Round walked with a swagger suggesting a high self-opinion. Six feet in height, with black hair and a moderately good physique, he had a tanned and clean-shaven face that would have been fairly handsome if it had not been for the cruelty in its lines. His clothing was more Mexican *vaquero and charro* than American cowhand in style. The hat was a fancy high-crowned *sombrero*. He had a frilly-bosomed, grubby white silk shirt, a necktie made from rattlesnake skin, a waist-long black *bolero* jacket and trousers with legs, which were tight on the thighs and wide at the bottom with silver filigree, ending in sharp-toed boots with large-roweled spurs that jingled loudly on high heels. However, his brown gunbelt was

8

Western in cut and carried two pearl-handled Colt Artillery Model Peacemaker revolvers in holsters that were tied down at the bottom.

Next to enter was Jack Straw, the oldest of the trio by several years. He was about an inch shorter than Round, whom he regarded with something close to a sardonic amusement although even one as touchy as Round would have been hard put to detect it. He was carrying instead of wearing a well-worn tan J.B. Stetson hat with a Montana peak indicative of his origins. His brown hair was cropped short and going gray at the temples, and his rugged, mustached face had the texture of old leather. His attire, the functional working garb of a cowhand from his home state, was nowhere nearly as flashy as that worn by Round. While plain, his gunbelt and brace of walnut-handled Peacemakers, which—while of different barrel lengths—hung just right for rapid withdrawal, had obviously seen much use.

Although not quite as tall and somewhat more lightly built than the other two, about halfway between them in age, the man who now called himself Haynes Lashricker was more impressive. Like Straw, he had his black Texas-style Stetson in his left hand. His neatly trimmed hair was black and his handsome, tanned face clean-shaven; his forehead, with a noticeable scar shaped like a flattened W, showed none of Round's openly bullying truculence. Rather, it had an indication of strength of will and intelligence mingled with bitterness in its lines. Neat and functional without being flashy or fussy, his clothing was such as a prosperous rancher might wear when working on the range. On each side of his black waistbelt in a Missouri-style holster was a fine-looking ivory-handled Colt Pocket Pistol of Navy Caliber revolver—rechambered to accept metallic cartridges—with its butt turned forward so as to be readily accessible to either hand.

"This is Taos Lightning," Steel introduced, indicating the youngest man.

"They call me that 'cause I hail from there 'n' am," Round announced in what he considered to be a tough tone. His accent was common to New Mexico.

Swaggering across the room, watched with a less-than-flattering gaze by the other two visitors, the young man helped himself to a drink from the decanter on the dressing table. Then he took a cigar from the box next to it, bit off the end, and spat the removed portion on to the floor. Having established himself as being particularly tough and competent, he lounged against the wall to puff smoke rings into the air with studied ease.

"Jack Straw," Steel continued in a brittle tone.

"Mind if I get me a drink and smoke, gents?" the oldest of the trio inquired, and waited for an answer in the affirmative before doing so.

"And _Hayden_ Lashricker," Steel continued. His attitude suggested that he had left the best and most important of his selection until last, but also that the alteration to the Christian name was not made by mistake. It had long been his practice to learn everything he could about whomever he was hiring in the hope of acquiring information useful in ensuring that his will could be imposed as a result of it. "Will you take a drink and smoke, Mr. Lashricker?"

"No, thank you," the last of the trio replied in a Southern drawl indicative of a good education. If he had noticed the supposed mistake in his name when he was announced, he gave no sign of it. "I'd rather hear why you've asked us to come here."

"To handle something for us," Steel replied. His tone implied that he had said all that was necessary.

"And what would that 'something' be?" Lashricker queried with no discernible change in his unemotional tone.

"Dealing with some people who don't share our interests," Blair put in. He did not want it to appear that his nondescript partner was the leader of their organization.

"Stop this pussyfooting around and tell us who it is we'll be up against," the Southron commanded in the same flat and unemotional fashion.

"Does it matter?" Norman growled, his motives for speaking the same as those of Blair.

"It does to *me*," Lashricker affirmed. "I choose when—and *who*—I fight!"

"You'll be up against a retired Cavalry officer, Major Wilson Eardle for one," Norman supplied with a scowl, knowing military men tended to stand by one another in and out of the service.

"And who else?" the Southron queried, the other two professional gunfighters leaving him to do the talking although Round was clearly itching to speak.

"The sheriff of Spanish Grant County, most likely," Blair supplied.

"And who else?" Lashricker repeated with a

11

touch of asperity coming into his voice. "There *is* somebody else, isn't there?"

"An outfit called the Wedge," Steel supplied, knowing better than to provoke the Southron any further.

"Well, thank you for the offer, gentlemen," Lashricker said quietly, taking a small yet bulky buckskin pouch from his jacket's inside left breast pocket. He removed some of the money it contained and handed it to Steel. "I've already used some for traveling here, and this will cover me for my other expenses and time."

"You mean you're leaving?" Blair yelped.

"I mean just that," the Southron confirmed.

"Why?" Norman came as close as he dared to demanding.

"For personal reasons," Lashricker replied, and with a nod in the direction of Straw, walked out of the room, closing the door behind him.

"Damn it," Blair snarled. "We need him to be there ready to take over as the law in Child City either before or when sh—!"

The words trailed away as the speaker's partners glared at him in a prohibitive fashion. He realized he was saying too much about a part of their plans of which it was better the remaining pair of hired guns remained unaware.

"Hell, I can do *that* for you easy 'nough," Round claimed, although he had no idea what was entailed by the comment.

"We've something else in mind for you," Steel asserted.

"You're paying me," Round said with a shrug. However, he was eyeing the buckskin sack and noticing that, even with some of the contents removed, it was bulkier than the one in his possession. "Hell, though, I'm not surprised the beefhead got hisself cold feet all of a sudden. They do tell Doc Leroy's rides for the Wedge gave him that scar on his forehead 'n' has had him on the run for more'n a fair spell now."

"Are you gentlemen willing to stay on?" Steel asked, realizing that his position with his partners had been weakened by the departure of the man he had said was the best hired gun available for their purposes.

"I am," Straw asserted without emotion.

"Once Taos Lightning's in, he's in all the way, root hawg or die," Round declared in a bombastic fashion. "Only, I reckon's how it's only right 'n' square that Jack 'n' me split that money turned in by Lashricker, seeing as how we're going to do his share of whatever fighting's coming. So split her up even and say what you want for us to do."

Accepting that there was no other way to keep the services of the two men, who—while not up to the standard of the departed Southron—would each be able to exert control over any other hired guns, Steel grudgingly agreed without consulting his partners. Watching him divide the money returned by Lashricker, the other two began to think that they might find dealing with the new owners of the two ranches a different and far more difficult proposition than handling the original four had been—in the opening stages, at least. With the money matters concluded, the nondescript-looking partner outlined what he wanted done in Spanish Grant County without making any mention of the task that should have been assigned to Lashricker.

DO YOU KNOW WHO *SHE* IS?

"Howdy, Mrs. Eardle, Wils," Jethro "Stone" Hart greeted, stepping with a smile of welcome from the sidewalk in front of the Cattlemen's Bank in Child City. Stone was in his early thirties, just over six feet tall. There was a suggestion of strength in his wiry frame, and although his speech and attire were those of a cowhand from Texas, he still retained something of a soldier's straight-backed posture. Nevertheless, the ivory-handled Colt Civilian Model Peacemaker revolver in the open-topped, carefully contoured holster of his gunbelt hung just right for a fast draw and gave the appearance of having been used for that purpose on more than one occasion. He was black-haired, and his otherwise handsome face was marred by a long scar down his right cheek.

"I'm pleased to meet you, ma'am."

"You won't be unless you start calling me April," the woman answered cheerfully after bringing the fringe-topped surrey drawn by a spirited bay gelding to a halt. Five feet eight in height, she was a maturely beautiful woman, although no longer in the first flush of youth. The boss of the newly formed Wedge ranch suspected that, like his wife, she had taken especial care about the appearance she presented for the first visit to the seat of Spanish Grant County. Under her Wavelean hat, her blond hair was immaculately coiffured in a style that was attractive yet not fussy. While elegant in style and cut, her two-piece dove-gray traveling outfit was clearly functional. The jewelry she wore, while obviously valuable, was neither ostentatious in its size nor of such quantity that it would arouse envy from the female members of the community she was going to meet. All in all, she had the appearance of one long used to mingling with and making herself pleasant regardless of the company in which she found herself. Descending while speaking, she stepped onto the sidewalk with her right hand extended and continued, "If you don't, I'll have Wils go back to calling you Captain Hart."

"And she's mean enough to do it, Stone," warned Major Wilson Eardle, owner of the AW ranch, swinging from the Cheyenne roll rig of his big roan American five-gaited saddle horse with the ease of the cavalry officer he had been prior to his retirement.

His removal of the black Burnside campaign hat, which was the only sign of his past military career, showed he had close-cropped iron-gray hair. His face, florid because its texture would never take a tan, had a rugged strength and indicated he would be a man to reckon with in any circumstances. He had adopted the garments frequently used by many members of his social position and occupation in Arizona. The gunbelt around his waist had been service issue, but the high-riding cavalry holster had been converted to an open-topped style that allowed him to remove the walnut-handled Colt Cavalry Model Peacemaker with greater facility. Bowing in a gallant fashion, although knowing the movement could not be seen by the person to whom the gesture was directed, he went on, "Your servant, Mrs. Hart, ma'am."

"If you was my servant, I'd fire you for calling me *that*," Margaret Hart declared with a smile and a drawl that matched that of her husband. About the same age as Stone and five feet seven, she was good-looking, although she could not match the beauty or quality of attire of April Eardle. Clearly she, too, had taken considerable care with her appearance: She had on a white J.B. Stetson hat in the fashion of the Lone Star State from beneath the broad brim of which showed some of her curly tawny hair. Plain blue in color and made of inexpensive material, her dress could not entirely hide her neatly rounded slender physique. The dark spectacles she had on and the specially designed harness on the big Chesapeake Bay retriever seated at her left side gave indications that she was blind. In spite of this, and much to April Eardle's surprise, she accepted the hand that had been instinctively held her way and gave it a warm shake. "Or perhaps this husband of mine, being the Southern gentleman of the old school that he is, forgot to mention I have a Christian name?"

As was only to be expected, the first appearance in town by two families who had taken ranches in the county was the source of much interest to everybody in the town. Their coming had been preceded by the less dignified and much more rowdy arrival of members of each crew. Although there was clearly a certain amount of rivalry between the two groups— the AW riders were from various parts of the

Northern cattle-raising states and those of the Wedge were all Texans—it was on a friendly basis. Although three of the latter group had gone into Clitheroe's General Emporium next to the bank, the remainder had headed for Angus McTavish's Arizona State Saloon and were already within its hospitable doors.

However, it was the owners of the ranches and their wives who were of most interest to the assembled members of the population. Everybody present was in some way concerned with the various business interests, either directly or through membership in the respective families; they realized that the newcomers would be a not inconsiderable factor in future profits. All of the male representatives of the major concerns who could make it were gathered, and those who could not attend for some reason relied either upon their wives or junior partners to make the acquaintanceship upon which their future relationship with the Wedge and AW ranches would to a great extent depend.

Although the male portion of the crowd tended to gather in cliques formed either through similar or conflicting interests, the distaff side was divided roughly into two groups. Better-dressed than the other section, who were clearly from a lower stratum of society—although they also qualified as "good" women by the standards of the West, the female workers in the saloon and those from the discreet "house of ill repute" just clear of the outskirts were wisely absent—all members of the Child City Civic Betterment League, who considered themselves a most important factor in the town, held somewhat aloof from the rest of the crowd.

Nevertheless, they wished to see how the wives of the ranchers dressed and behaved before offering their acceptance. If the way they were looking was any guide, they found nothing to which they might take exception in the appearance of Margaret and April.

Before the amiable introductory conversation between the two families could be continued, there was an interruption.

"Hey, Ric!" a harsh voice with an Illinois accent said, much more loudly than was necessary to be heard by the man to whom the words were addressed. "Do you know who *she* is?"

"I surely do," declared the recipient of the question, his voice showing similar origins and having an equally hard timbre. "It's—!"

Having an idea of what was coming, April stiffened. A glance at her husband informed her that he had reached the same conclusion. However, the name was not spoken.

"A *real* good friend of mine, *hombre*!" announced a baritone voice with the drawl of a well-educated Texan before any more could be said.

"And *mine*, comes to that!" came a voice whose tenor tone was also clearly that of another son of the Lone Star State, albeit one who had not received as much schooling.

Swinging around with cold scowls intended to convey a hard menace on their poorly shaven and unprepossessing features, David Blunkett and Richard Haigh looked as mean as winter-starved grizzly bears fresh out from hibernation. Equally big and burly, they wore clothes that

18

might have struck somebody who was not conversant with the West as being that of cowhands. However, just about everybody in hearing and seeing range knew without needing to be told that such was not the way they earned their living. Rather, their living came from applying their strength or their low-hanging revolvers as a means of enforcing the will of their employers upon others. Having come to Child City with specific instructions to carry out, they had no liking for what was clearly an attempt to prevent them from doing as they had been told and paid to do.

Neither hired man needed to look far, or think hard, before realizing who had intervened.

Having come from the Emporium in time to hear what was being said, stepping from the sidewalk, the one who had made the first interruption would have been very hard to miss in any company. Standing a good six feet three—even without the tan-colored, Texas-style Stetson with silver conchas on the leather band around its low crown, or the high-heeled, sharp-toed boots of equally expensive appearance—he had golden-blond hair and an almost classically handsome cast of features. Below them was a massive spread of shoulders tapering to a narrow waist and opening to sturdy hips set on powerful, long legs. His clothes were those of a range-country dandy, and the fancily etched brown *buscadero* gunbelt about his midsection carried a matched brace of ivory-handled Colt Cavalry Model Peacemaker revolvers—their metalwork in that company's dark blue Best Citizen's finish—in tied-down holsters designed to permit a very rapid withdrawal in competent hands. Whether he could utilize this quality to its full advantage was not apparent.

Although lacking some three inches of the blond giant's height and possessing a physique that was lean as a steer fed in the greasewood country—however giving a suggestion of possessing an almost tireless strength—the second Texan was no less noticeable. His hair was short, and so black that it seemed to be dark blue in some lights, and his skin was so darkly tanned as to imply he had Indian blood. Although his features had an aura of almost babyish innocence, there was something in his red-hazel eyes that warned such was far from being his true nature. With the exception of the walnut grip of an aged Colt First Model of 1848 Dragoon revolver riding butt forward on the right and a massive ivory-handled bowie knife in a sheath at the left of his gunbelt, every item of clothing he had on—from hat to boots, which had lower heels than was *de rigueur* for a cowhand, although the rest of his garb suggested that this was his vocation—was black. He moved with a leisurely seeming fashion, yet seemed ready to burst into rapid action should that be required.

"Just who the hell asked you to come billing into something that's none of your goddamned nevermind?" Blunkett demanded, having his reputation for being wild, woolly, and full of fleas to consider, since it would prove useful for his future in the town.

"Didn't know we'd have to wait to be *asked*," the blond giant replied, giving not the slightest indication of being intimidated by the obviously threatening demeanor shown by both hard cases.

"Did I know such was going to be expected," the black-dressed Texas drawled dryly, suddenly no longer giving the impression of being young or innocent, "I just *might've* waited to get asked."

"Who the hell do you reckon you are?" Haigh snarled, motivated by the same thoughts as those of his companion.

"I don't *reckon* at all, having been around me since the day I was born," the blond giant answered, advancing with a steady stride until just beyond reaching distance of the two hard cases. "But, seeing as how you pair don't know, my name's Mark Counter."

"Which, you two being so all-fired nosy 'n' all," the black-dressed Texan went on, keeping pace with his companion, "I might as well come right on out 'n' confess, most shame-faced, as how on more 'n' one occasion I've been called the Ysabel Kid."

The introductions caused Blunkett and Haigh to exchange quick glances showing a mixture of surprise and disbelief. Although there had been no mention of either being involved in what they were sent to do, each of the names they had just heard was well known in its own right throughout the West and, via various accounts supplied in the blood-and-thunder books so popular there, even in the East. However, having been raised in the Northern states, neither of the hard cases wanted to give even partial credence to all the tales told about the qualities as fighting men par excellence Mark Counter or the Ysabel Kid possessed. There was another name, invariably given greater

21

prominence, that was almost always mentioned with them. However, scanning the crowd quickly—although a third Texan cowhand had followed them from the store—the hard cases concluded that one of such small size could not possibly be he.

Figuring that the odds were no more than one against one—even if they had to wonder just how much of the stories were true—each hard case still gave thought to the kind of reputation he must acquire among the town dwellers if he was to carry out the work that was coming in the near future.

"Yeah!" Blunkett said sarcastically as he darted a leering and knowing glance in April's direction. "I reckon you'd be sure to know somebody like h—!"

Even as Eardle was preparing to move forward, his face suffused by anger, he found he had no need to demonstrate his opposition to the way in which his wife was being treated and try to prevent a disclosure neither wanted to be made.

"Know her and am proud to, *hombre*!" Mark stated.

"Which same goes for me, *pelados*," the Kid seconded, using the Spanish work that, along the Rio Grande where he had spent most of his formative years, was employed to mean a corpse robber of the worst kind. "Only, Miz April might not want it knowed as how she'd even met somebody the likes of me once."

Advancing a pace while his *amigo* was speaking, instead of reaching for either Colt the blond giant swung his right arm with devastating speed. Although the blow he struck was with a flat palm and not a clenched fist, it proved just as effective. Caught on the cheek with a force far beyond anything he had ever experienced, before his grab at the butt of his revolver could come even close to completion, Blunkett was flung in a spinning arc to alight sprawling on the rutted surface of the street. As he landed, the weapon slid from his holster for a short distance.

Spitting out a profanity, although avenging the attack upon his companion was not his main motive, Haigh started to reach for his weapon an instant after it became apparent that hostile action was being taken by the blond giant. However, he achieved no greater success than had Blunkett. Furthermore, due to the response he produced and the person who provided it, he might have counted himself fortunate that nothing worse befell him. With a sensation of shock, he realized a change to more than the formerly easy Texas drawl had taken place. The approaching man no longer looked either young or innocent. Rather, his Indian-dark face had acquired the aspect of a full-blood brave-heart warrior on the warpath, hunting for the hated white-eye brother's scalp.

What was more, the bowie knife that seemed to materialize in the Kid's hand—its blade eleven and a half inches in length and two and a half inches wide—was approaching with what seemed to be the intention of sending the clip point home in a belly-ripping thrust!

At that moment, the third of the Texans to have emerged from the Emporium made his presence felt in no uncertain fashion. His height was no more than five feet six. With his black

Stetson dangling over his shoulders by its *barbiquejo* chin strap, his hair could be seen to be neatly trimmed and dusty blond. He was good-looking, although there was nothing eye-catching about his tanned face unless one made a closer scrutiny. Then it became apparent that there was a strength of will and maturity in its lines that seemed out of place with the rest of his appearance. While his clothing had obviously cost as much as that of the blond giant, he did not have the same flair for showing it to its best advantage. Rather, he gave the impression that the garments were castoffs from some larger and better-favored person. Nor did his excellently made gunbelt—with two bone-handled Colt Civilian Model Peacemakers in holsters designed for a cross-draw—seem to give any added stature. Nevertheless, closer inspection revealed that he had a physique as well developed as that of Mark.

Having watched all that was happening, the small Texan stiffened slightly as he saw the way the Kid was behaving.

"*Lon!*"

The single word uttered by the seemingly insignificant cowhand had the resonance of one who expected to have his words obeyed.

Strangely as it might have seemed on the surface, clearly the implication being understood, that was what happened!

Numbed by the sudden change that had come over his erstwhile young and innocent-seeming intended assailant into an immobility that could easily have proved fatal under the circumstances, Haigh could not make his hand do more than close about the butt of his Colt. However, on

hearing the word spoken by the small Texan—
or perhaps because his point of aim had never
been where it gave the impression of being—
the Kid changed it at the last moment. Instead
of the blade going home for a belly-ripping slash
that would have allowed an Indian warrior to
count coup and maybe take a scalp, the bowie
knife rose and the rounded brass pommel of the
hilt slammed between the hard case's eyes.
Stunned by the impact and with blood running
from the gash that was made, the hard case
toppled backward to alight spread-eagled a short
distance from his companion.

I WAS APRIL HOSMAN AND I WORKED IN SALOONS

"Leave it be, feller!" commanded a voice with
an authoritative ring in its New England accent as David Blunkett made a reaching motion toward the Colt Artillery Model
Peacemaker revolver that had slipped from his
holster when he was knocked down. "Mark
Counter treated you gentle first time, so I don't
want to have him get *riled* and stop doing it."

Sheriff Amon Reeves stepped from where he
had been on the point of leaving the group of
men with whom he was watching the arrival
of the two families, having intended to inter-
vene with the hard cases if the matter had not
been taken from his hands before he could make
a start. He was tall and well, if not bulkily, built.
Despite his accent, his attire was that of a working cowhand and of a quality that implied he
did not add to his salary through corruption

of any kind. He was, in fact, regarded by the cowhands who were practically his only source of business—and then only on a very minor scale—as being a fair-minded and impartial peace officer, always ready to do his duty in the most most amiable and gentle way possible. But he was capable, if necessary, of using harder methods with either his bare fists or the walnut-handled Peacemaker in the holster on his right thigh.

"You pair got any special business in town?" the sheriff went on as soon as his order was obeyed.

"Nope," Blunkett lied sullenly, sitting up and glowering at the blond giant.

"Then, was I you," Reeves stated. "I'd take your buddy to see Doc Gottlinger to have his head 'tended, then the pair of you can head for any place where you might be more welcome than you are here. Was I asked, I'd say the chore you came for is over."

"You don't have no right—!" Blunkett began as he returned the revolver to his holster without attempting to clean away the dust from the street, trying to recover something of the reputation for hardness he had hoped to create. He seemed puzzled by the suggestion that his latest employment was already at an end.

"So have some liber-rad softshell at the territorial capital write to one of his kind's newspapers about it, like they're allus so eager to do," Reeves suggested dryly and with no sign of relenting. "Only, do it after you've shaken the dust of my bailiwick from your boots. Or do you want to take it any further?"

"Nope!" Blunkett gritted, hoping his employers did not hear of his failure. "Come on, Ric, let's get your head 'tended, then ride out."

"Just a moment, Sheriff!" April Eardle put in after the hard cases had walked away followed by an obviously disgruntled Doctor Klaus Gottlinger, who would far rather have preferred to remain. She was standing stiff as a board, her beautiful face set in lines of grim determination, as she looked toward the assembled people. She raised her voice to project it as she had learned to do while working as a top-grade entertainer in saloons. "Ladies and gentlemen. I would like to say something, if I can have your attention for a few seconds, please."

"There's no need for *that*, dear!" Major Wilson Eardle declared, knowing what his wife had in mind.

"Yes, there is, Wils," the blonde corrected. Then she turned her gaze so it scanned the crowd, who, particularly the members of the Child City Civic Betterment League, were staring with rapt attention. Her demeanor was completely calm, but there was a suggestion of anxiety in her voice as she continued, "I think you should all know that, as those pair were figuring on telling you, before I married Wilson, I was April Hosman and I worked in saloons."

There was a rumble of barely audible talk at the declaration.

The words served to establish how the relationship between the Eardle and Hart families would continue.

Knowing something of the attitudes to be expected in small towns, having grown up in and around one before leaving Texas with her husband to make their new home in Spanish

27

Grant County, Margaret Hart caught Stone's arm and gave it a gentle tug. Knowing what was required by the gesture, the boss of the Wedge ranch gently took his wife by the right biceps and guided her from the sidewalk until they stood alongside the blonde. As soon as she moved, her big Chesapeake Bay retriever advanced as it was trained to do. It halted briefly at the edge of the sidewalk as she did, despite the guidance being offered by her husband. Stepping onto the street, it allowed height to be gauged by its mistress's hold upon the handle of the harness it wore. When she had satisfied herself upon the point, she descended without difficulty and continued to move in the required direction.

It was soon apparent to the onlookers that the Harts were not alone in the action they were taking. Not unexpectedly, Eardle had already advanced until standing in a challenging fashion near April. Nor were the two cowhands who had intervened slower to respond in kind. They were closely followed by a buxom young woman who had arrived in a buggy accompanying the Wedge crew but was precluded because of her sex and "good" reputation from joining them in the saloon. Bareheaded, her ash-blonde hair drawn back tightly into a bun, she carried a suggestion of rugged independence about her good-looking, slightly aquiline features. The gingham dress she wore gave an indication that the hourglass contours of her body were not produced by artificial means, and she moved her five-foot-four body with a lightness that implied she was far from being puny.

Coming from in front of Clitheroe's General

Emporium, the diminutive dusty-blond whose one word had saved Richard Haigh from at least an incapacitating injury added to the number offering unqualified support for the blonde in the face of any opposition toward her on account of the way in which she had earned her living in the past. However, the Texan no longer gave the impression of being small. In fact, such was the strength of his personality that he conveyed a sensation of being the largest person present.

To the people of Child City watching what was taking place, one thing was all too apparent. Regardless of who and what she had been in the past, April Eardle had a number of good friends who were willing to stand by her regardless of what public opinion elsewhere might be. Every one of them could be accounted as being a person of importance either to the town or elsewhere. That was especially the case with the dusty-blond.

There was an almost tangible tension as each member of the local population waited with bated breath for somebody else to make the first remark. All of them realized how much the future of the town depended on what happened next. It was clear that the Harts were solidly aligned with the Eardles, and that an affront to April would be considered as also striking the Texan couple. Mark Counter and the Ysabel Kid had already stated and all too convincingly demonstrated where their sympathies lay, without needing to comment further. Whatever theories might have been formed as to the possible reason why they were giving their unswerving support to a woman who claimed to have worked in saloons were of no concern to them.

Nor, even though he was a resident in neither the town nor the Arizona Territory, was the just as obvious support by Dusty Fog ignored.

The effect of arousing resentment from the two families would only be at the local level, and was reduced to some extent by there being no closer source of supply for all major commodities their ranches would require. On the other hand, because of his close connections with General Jackson Baines "Ole Devil" Hardin—a major force to be reckoned with in the affairs of the Lone Star State and able to apply influence even in Washington, D.C.—the *big* young Texan was reputed to have access to many of the highest social and political levels, and not just in his home state. It was rumored that he had the ear of the governor of Arizona, and he certainly was on excellent terms with Colonel Myles Raines of Backsight, well-known to be the coming man in the policies of the Territory and one of those especially concerned in the attempts to attain statehood. Such a person could not be dismissed lightly, and he was certain to have a great loyalty to all whom he regarded as his friends.

Despite being aware of the ramifications that might accrue should the response prove unfavorable to the group standing in the street with an aura of defiance, none of the assembled men wished to take the lead in responding. The only one who would have been in the fore without hesitation had decided that his business association as attorney for both ranchers—and as their supporter through all the problems that arose as a result of the Wedge crew—debarred him from making the opening move. Those who were married wanted to get an inkling of how their wives felt on the subject before committing themselves, and even the single members of the crowd were anxious to wait until this was made clear.

After about thirty seconds, the silence was broken.

"Well, now," Mrs. Flora Sutherland said, stepping forward. The Highland burr in her voice was for once as accentuated as that of her husband when he was celebrating Burns' Night with all the fervor of a Scot far from his native home. Gray-haired, she was tall, slim without being gaunt, and her freckled face had a warm charm. "I've a cousin on Edward's side of the family who married a Sassenach, but I don't hold *that* against her. Will you ladies come and take something with the Child City Civic Betterment League at my home?"

"And a terrible expense that's going to be for me," Counselor Edward Sutherland groaned to the owner of the Emporium, who stood near him in the crowd, despite being amused and pleased by the way in which his wife had taken the lead in the affair. Short and giving the impression of being chubby, although his rotundity was rubbery firm flesh, he had sun-reddened features that gave him an appearance of being far more ingenuous than was the case. His Bostonian tones took on a similar timbre to that of his wife as he went on, "Now I don't suppose you would—?"

"You don't suppose right," Amos Clitheroe

confirmed with a grin, knowing the words were no more than he had expected to hear. "You're spending too much time around Angus McTavish, and his tightfisted ways're starting to rub off on you, although I think they were always there."

"I'd be delighted to come," April replied with a heartfelt warmth, since she knew the invitation was an open declaration that her past was not going to be held against her where at least one member of the community was concerned. "How about you, Margaret?"

"I'd love to," the mistress of the Wedge ranch confirmed, and indicated the ash-blonde. "By the way, this is my nurse and good friend, Steffie Willis. Can she come along with us, please?"

"Of course," Mrs. Sutherland assented immediately and with genuine warmth, although some of the others—but not all, by any means—were clearly trying to prevent their reservations on the point from becoming too obvious.

"I must say I like your outfit, Mrs. Eardle," Mrs. Emma Clitheroe declared, as plump and jolly looking as her husband. Wanting to show off her knowledge of such matters, since they formed the main portion of her side of their business, she continued, "It's Selina of Polveroso, isn't it?"

"Well, yes, it is," the blonde admitted. She had hoped the point would not be noticed, much less mentioned, since the woman named was famous throughout the West for the excellent quality and high prices of her garments. Wanting to carry the matter off lightly so that she did not arouse envy or hostility among those present who were unable to afford such costly attire, she went on, "When I told Wils what he had paid for it, he said I got it for a ridiculous figure."

"Why, you have a wond—!" Mrs. Clitheroe commenced indignantly, then realized what was implied by the play on words and burst into a merry laugh, concluding with, "A ridiculous figure indeed."

"My Edward always tells me the same, no matter how cheap I pay," Mrs. Sutherland claimed after the merriment had swept through all save a couple of frosty-faced elderly members of the League. "But he would, even if I had the misfortune to have a figure like yours, Mrs.—!"

"April," the blonde suggested. "The whales must hate me, the way I get it."

"I'm surprised there are any whales left for anybody else after they'd been used for *me*," claimed the largest of the local women, who was clearly suffering from the constriction applied by a girdle made from the bones of that sea creature. "What we girls do for men."

"And they never show any gratitude for all our efforts," complained the smallest and youngest of the group, who showed signs of being in a late stage of pregnancy.

"My Stone does," Margaret stated to keep the good humor going. "Because I always tell him he has to."

"Whoo!" Sutherland breathed as the women took their departure. "That went off much more smoothly than I dared to hope for, particularly after what those two hard cases tried to do."

"The Texans soon enough put a stop to that," Clitheroe replied. "I could almost feel the slap young Counter gave his man myself."

"If you ask me," Sutherland said somberly, "the other's lucky he's still alive. If Cap'n Fog hadn't yelled, the Kid was likely to cut him from belly to neck. Come on, 'Mos. I think the time is ripe for us to go and greet our rancher friends properly." Having led the businessmen forward and presented them to Stone and Eardle, the three members of what he called "General Hardin's floating outfit," he continued, "And now, if you gentlemen want my considered opinion—!"

"We *don't!*" chorused all the assembled locals. It was well known to them that—as proof of his canny Scottish descent—the stocky attorney invariably announced that his "considered opinion" amounted to a professional consultation and required payment by either a drink of the best Scotch whisky available or a good-class cigar.

"Well, I'll take a chance on it," Eardle declared. "How about you, Stone?"

"Why, surely so," the boss of the Wedge ranch agreed. "My attorney can always prove insanity when I get sued and taken before the local justice of the peace for not paying any consultant fee."

"Ignoring that, although I won't hesitate to sue," Sutherland said in his most judicial fashion, although his legal duties had never been overextensive despite there being no other attorney in Spanish Grant County. "In my considered opinion, gentlemen, we should sojourn

34

to yon jovial wayside tavern and drink to one another's health."

"Now, there's what I consider a real good considered opinion," Stone claimed. "So, like we used to say when we was starting a trail drive, let's head 'em up and move 'em out."

Unbeknownst to the men until later, there were dramatic developments for the town's ladies shortly after they had crowded into the substantial sitting room of the attorney's home. With the house so near to the edge of the town, Margaret had removed the harness from Rollo—as the Chesapeake Bay retriever was called—and turned him loose, knowing she could do so in safety. She knew he would indulge in his natural instinct to go hunting, although this was no longer restricted to fetching back waterfowl shot on the wing by hunters, and would return when summoned by a blast on the whistle she carried in her handbag. With the dog gone, she needed some assistance from Steffie until she was established on a seat, there to have all her other wants filled by various members of the League.

"Oh, Lord!" Matilda Canoga, the smallest member of the group, suddenly croaked and, clasping at her midsection, she flopped limply on to a chair. "I—I—I'm getting to feel real *strange!*"

"You better take a look, Steffie," Margaret suggested, aware by her other senses, which had become sharpened through the loss of her sight, that the ash-blonde had remained close by ready to serve her in any way that was needed.

"Hmmph!" Steffie grunted, having passed

35

through the other women with a deft ease and given Matilda a professional going-over. She had been a trained nurse before marrying Rusty Willis of the Wedge, whom she had met while he was under her care in the hospital after taking a bad throw from a horse. "You're going into labor."

"Oh, God!" Matilda screeched, guessing what the term implied even though it was her first pregnancy and she had not been given any instruction as to what feelings to expect. "Get Toby and the doctor!"

"If Toby's your husband, he's better off wherever he is right now, especially if he's propping up a bar with the rest of the shiftless menfolks, which is all they're good for anytime and even more at times like *this*," the ash-blonde claimed with a cheery self-confidence that the would-be mother found most reassuring. "And I've always been taught that a doctor's less use than decoration at a delivery. Get some water to boiling, ladies. Mrs. Sutherland, is there some place I can put my patient to bed?"

"Of course," the attorney's wife confirmed without hesitation. "Carry her into the guest bedroom some of you."

"Carry *nothing*!" Steffie denied. "She's as strong as a bull pup and the walk will do her good. Come on, girl, up on your feet and let's get her done."

"Does your friend know what she's doing, Mrs. Hart?" one of the older women asked worriedly. "After all, Matilda is my daughter-in-law."

"And she'll pretty soon be making you a proud grandmomma who'll spoil the baby ev-

36

ery which way," Margaret declared. "Because Steffie's delivered more than one baby into the world and she's never lost one—or a mother—yet."

"Sure you can lend a hand, honey," the ash-blonde assented in response to the only unmarried member of the League who had offered her services. "Have you ever done it before?"

"Well—no," the volunteer admitted in a shamefaced fashion.

"Then just keep one thing in mind," Steffie said with a reassuring grin and a gentle squeeze at the other's biceps. "If you decide to swoo a swoon, which I don't reckon you will, make sure you fall backwards and not across the momma. That's what I was told my first time, and it's mighty good advice to follow."

After the mother-to-be had been moved and all except the young volunteer removed from the scene by Steffie, an awkward lull developed among the remaining women. However, it was quickly brought to an end by April's putting to use the training she had had as an entertainer in saloons. Of course, she could not use the kind of material that had done so well with her all male audiences. Nevertheless, she produced a number of anecdotes involving names that were well known to her audience and these brought smiles from the majority of the women.

Continuing to put her extensive knowledge of human nature to use, the blonde also contrived to win over two frosty-faced elderly spinsters who had been the least responsive to the prospect of her company by seeking their advice on various matters to which she claimed no knowledge. She drew laughter—not scorn, which might earlier have been her lot—when she asserted that her cooking was so bad the utensils ran and hid whenever she entered the kitchen. However, she declared, she was willing to bet she was the only one present who could burn water when attempting to boil it.

Nor was Margaret unable to help relieve the tension. She prevented any embarrassment from being experienced when questioned about how she was able to cope so well with her disability. Having estimated Mrs. Clitheroe's height and weight—dropping a few pounds deliberately, everyone suspected—the mistress of the Wedge did the same with two other women of diverse size. Directing a smile around the room, April took a seat before requesting that she be the next subject. Deducing what had happened, to the amusement of everybody—including the blonde—Margaret turned the tables neatly on her by giving her correct height with the proviso that she was not speaking through just below her bosom.

By the time an eight-pound baby boy was delivered, with both he and his mother in the best of health, there was a great accord among all the women present. Even those who had had reservations over the propriety of allowing Steffie in their company were now lavish in their praise for her ability.

Although nobody present envisaged the possibility, the birth was to have a salutary effect elsewhere in the not too far distant future.

I HEAR TELL AS HOW YOU'RE A *KILLER*

Unaware of what was happening at the welcome meeting given by the Child City Civic Betterment League for the wives of the ranchers and Steffie Willis—now having been elevated considerably in social standing as a result of her activities as an extemporized midwife—some of the rest of Spanish Grant County's male population were already enjoying themselves at the Arizona State saloon although as yet few of the residents of Child City were present unless employed there to serve drinks or clean up around the main barroom.

The scene was much as could have been witnessed on payday in any town throughout the cattle-raising country of the West, or—albeit probably in a more rowdy and extravagant fashion due to the extra money received—at those that served as shipping points for the trail herds brought to Kansas.

Except in minor details, the requirements of cowhands in town did not vary much. Despite each being a rugged individualist, he preferred to have others from the ranch to which he gave his loyalty—after having, if only literally, thrown his bedroll into the chuckwagon—somewhere around. On the other hand, because living in close proximity to the other members of the crew tended to sharpen his wits, he wanted to try them out against new opposition. This could best be achieved in the smoke-filled environs of a saloon, probably with a few more drinks of hard liquor than might be deemed advisable and the rough-and-tumble feminine company most of these places provided as an added stimulant. The women employed in a "house of ill repute" were seen as supplying a different, albeit equally imperative, need in a land where "good" female companionship was extremely limited and usually beyond the reach of the cowhand. Should the end result of a session in a saloon be a bare-fisted brawl, with weapons confined to pieces of furniture, the visit to town was deemed an even greater success.

Since a horse, saddle, and a gun were among the most necessary of every cowhand's worldly possessions, they tended to be featured prominently in his leisure activities outdoors. This sometimes led to wild riding and indiscriminate shooting—on the streets generally into the air or at inanimate objects, although headgear that differed from the norm might prove an irresistible attraction—as he and his companions sought to demonstrate their abilities. Yet they would all experience remorse if any innocent person should be injured as a result of such reckless behavior, and they generally paid to the afflicted whatever recompense their means allowed.

The cowhands who were gathered, many of them members of the Wedge and AW crews, were out to enjoy themselves to the full. Still, out of respect for Sheriff Amon Reeves's fair yet firm treatment and deference to the orders received from their bosses prior to heading for Child City, they intended to keep their fun and frolics within the stipulated bounds even though neither Waggles Harrison, nor Jimmy Conlin, *segundos* of the two ranches respectively, was present to help serve as a restraining influence. Also having been given the same instructions by the foremen who were running things in behalf of the late owners until the fate of the Arrow P and Vertical Triple E spreads was settled, those members of each who were present were just as willingly prepared to adhere to the required standards of behavior.

The arrival of the two bosses and a number of influential citizens might have served as a pall on the festivities had it not been for the foresight shown by the owner of the saloon. Realizing that the situation was going to arise, since he kept the only premises of the kind in Spanish Grant County—the large adobe cantina run by the owner of the vast property for the benefit of his *vaqueros* having closed and been deserted after his death and their departure back to Mexico—Angus McTavish had circumvented it by setting up a smaller yet just as adequately equipped room at the rear. This had soon become accepted as an area in which the leaders of the community could relax in the company of their peers.

Although the United States was a land that boasted the principle of all men being created equal, the idea of a separate area for different levels of society was welcomed by all concerned. The general consensus of opinion was that the hired hands did not want the boss around while they were whooping things up, regardless of how popular and well-liked he might be. Nor did employers like Stone Hart and Major Wilson Eardle, sharing a very shrewd judgment of human nature that no liberal ever attained, wish

41

to have the enjoyment of their men constrained by their continued presence. It was a point of view with which the officers from Fort Mescalero just beyond the county line—who also added to the custom drawn in by McTavish—were in complete accord when visiting Child City. Not that there had ever been any attempt to enforce the segregation in any way; it was completely on a voluntary basis.

Walking across the barroom with the rest of the party, Stone glanced around. He noticed that, in addition to the local cowhands and members of his crew who had come in, there were half a dozen soldiers at one table. The leathery-faced corporal who was the senior of them turned his head away for some reason after glancing toward the newcomers. At another table were a quartet of hard-looking men who, despite being younger and somewhat cleaner in appearance, Stone guessed to be the same kind as the pair with whom Mark Counter and the Ysabel Kid had dealt in the street. He wondered what they were doing in town, and assumed they could have been brought in by the late Eustace Edgar Eisteddfod to help make trouble between the Wedge and AW ranches. Concluding that they were none of his concern, he greeted his hands; Eardle did likewise with those from the AW. Then each of them instructed the bartenders to put up drinks for the house and followed the rest of the group into the back room.

Appearances did not lie.

The quartet who had been the first of the noncowhands to catch the attention of the Wedge ranch were all hired guns. However,

Stone was wrong in his assumption that they had been sent for by the man he knew as Eisteddfod and had arrived too late to play whatever part was intended for them. Instead, they had been recruited by Michael Round to work for the trio of conspirators who had actually been behind the supposed Welshman, and were in Child City to carry out the orders he had given to them. All were of about the same height and build, and all wore range-style clothing of various quality that was alike in never having been used for working cattle.

"Might as well make a start at earning our pay, fellers," said Jamie Cann. Red-haired, he was the most expensively attired of the group and had appointed himself their leader.

"Who're we going to push first?" Harold Best queried. He was ugly, going bald, and the shortest and oldest of the party.

"How's about that beefhead kid's doing all the talking over there," suggested Thomas Terry, who was swarthy and not too clean, but fancied himself as exceptionally tough and fast with a gun. "Do you know who he is?"

"No," Cann admitted. "Why would we?"

"He's the one took out Skinny McBride," Terry explained.

"I heard such'd come off, but making wolf bait of that scrawny son of a bitch wouldn't take no special heap of doing," Cann commented, although he could see the implications of the information. "At his *best*, he warn't what I'd call a good man with a gun. How'd it happened?"

"I wasn't hereabouts to see," Terry admitted. "But I met up with one of those fellers come with Jer Korbin and he told me about it. Seems the Skin tried to take him one night outside here and, when the smoke cleared, damned if it wasn't a case of slow for Skinny."

"Why not take that black-dressed beefhead's come in with the big fancy-dressed cuss 'n' the short runt's've gone into the back room?" John Birt asked. The youngest of the hard cases, this was his first employment of such a nature; he had been obtained because he was Cann's cousin. Having frequently been made conscious of his inexperience by the others, he was growing a beard in an attempt to make himself seem older. "He looks like he's a 'breed 'n' no mean-er'n a babe in arms."

"That's how he *looks* for sure," Best conceded in a coldly derisive tone, never hesitating to show his far greater knowledge over Birt in the hope of undermining Cann's assumption of leader-ship. "Only, I'd like to have ten simoleons for every man who's died through taking looks for beings."

"Who is he, 'Rold?" Terry queried. He was inclined to favor the swarthy hard case over Cann.

"The Ysabel Kid," Best replied. "I heard tell as how he was hereabouts with Dusty Fog 'n' Mark Counter. That must've been Fog who went to mix with the high mucky-mucks in the back, but I don't know just where 'n' how the short-growed runt figures in it—Less'n he's some-body's poor kin who has to be found a chore."

"That cagey son of a bitch Mike Round never said nothing about them three being in the game," Cann said grimly. He knew the trio of names ranked high in the annals of Western gun-handling and were not calculated to fill most who heard it with enthusiasm over the prospect of having to lock horns with them. Choosing to ignore the reference that concluded the previous remark, although he—like the others—knew it was aimed at himself and Birt, he went on in a commanding fashion, "Still, seeing as we've took pay for it, we'll have to do what we was telled. You want to get it started, Tom?"

"Well, I *could* easy 'nough," Terry answered. "But I reckon as how it'd be good practice for Johnny-boy here."

"All right," Birt said as the eyes of Terry and Best studied him in a mocking fashion. Having acquired some skill at handling his low-hanging Colt Civilian Model Peacemakers, he was confident he could do everything that was necessary. He was eager to acquire the reputation of being a killer for the first time. "I'll do it!"

"Give him cause to take you on," Cann instructed. "Then we'll back your play when you've got her done."

"I tell you gentlemen from Texas as how we've got us the world's biggest, meanest, 'n' smartest rattlers back home to Walla Walla, Washington," announced a lanky young member of the AW crew in the center of several cowhands around his age. He did not come from either the town or the state to which he referred, but had decided the name had a better ring than Bedford, Massachusetts, from where he originated. "Why, Momma couldn't raise no cherries for us kids 'cause said rattlers kept a-biting of her trees. Then they used to just sit back 'n' wait for birds to eat the cherries, 'n' drop dead from the pizen so as they could get a meal without needing to go crawling 'round 'n' hunting for the sucker."

"Well, now, Sammywell," Oswald "Thorny" Bush of the Wedge drawled in a way that—in addition to his clothing—established that he was from the Lone Star State. He had turned eighteen three days earlier. He was tall and slim, and had filled out quite a bit from the excellent cooking of Chow Willicka since taking on with the trail drive that brought the cattle to their new home. What was more, he had matured under the guidance of the men with whom he had associated and reached the point where, although none would have admitted it to him, they deemed he had attained the honored status of having "made a hand." Part of the growing-up process had been to gain a reputation for telling jokes, and he knew he was now faced with a challenge to better the one supplied by a rival. "Them's tolerable smart rattlers, I'll give you. Only, they don't come up to our'n back to home in Waxahachie. Why, one time an itty-bitty young 'n' fresh out'n its momma bit the tongue of our chuckwagon. Damned if that ole tongue didn't swell up so fast, we had to unhitch to save the rest of the wagon from dying of the pizen."

"Lordy Lord, fellers," Jason Willis said with a tolerant grin, looking toward the youngsters from the spot where he and several men of more advanced years had gathered. About five feet ten, with a sturdy build, he was ruggedly good-looking and had hair of a red hue that accounted for his nickname, "Rusty." Clearly married life suited him, for his clothes were more tidy than they were in his bachelor days. He still wore

46

his walnut handled Colt Artillery Model Peace-maker in a low-hanging draw, though he would never claim to be real fast with it. Like Peaceful Gunn and Silent Churchman, he was an original member of the Wedge crew from the days when they were engaged in taking herds of cattle to Kansas on contract to ranchers who preferred the business handled that way. Tonight, he had elected to stay on at the spread to help the *segundo* handle some chores. However, he had been ordered by Steffie to come with the rest so nobody would think he was henpecked, even though the two of them knew he was. "Do you reckon we was ever that young?"

"I dunno about the rest of you," the Ysabel Kid drawled, having always asserted that he preferred to stop with the common folks instead of mixing with the high mucky-mucks in the back room like his two *amigos,* "but I still am."

"There's some who'd say you was born *old,* Lon," stated the dandy-dressed cowhand currently working with the Wedge known only as Dude. " 'Specially in sinful doings, or don't-ings."

At that moment something happened to bring the cheerful conversation to an end.

The quartet of hard cases had left their table and walked toward the bar, Birt slightly ahead of the other three. The route they took led them to where the younger cowhands were gathered. As his companions came to a halt, the youngest of them moved forward a short distance, throwing a grin their way.

"They reckon as you can allus tell a Texas beefhead by the loudmouthed bragging he

47

does," Birt said loudly, hooking his right thumb over his gunbelt close to the butt of his Colt in a position of readiness. "And I've never heard so much of it afore as I just now did. 'Course, there's some's might say I shouldn't mention it, seeing's how I hear tell's how you're a killer. Only, that don't scare me none."

At the words, the group of younger cowhands turned. Taking notice of the way in which the speaker was standing, they all sensed trouble coming. What was more, although there were three other hard cases standing behind the one who had made the insulting remarks, all were facing away in a manner that suggested they had no part in whatever their companion was contemplating. That made the matter personal between him and Bush. Therefore, although they all had a liking for the Wedge hand—who was a year, at least, younger than all of them—they knew he must stand or fall on his own resources. Nor, they felt certain, would he want it any other way. With that thought in mind, they drew aside until he was left in the clear.

Although they were watching and listening with interest, the Kid and the older men a short distance away knew they could not intercede in the youngster's behalf as long as the affair remained restricted to himself and the skinny young hard case.

"There's no need why it should, *hombre*," Bush said quietly, thinking without pleasure of the previous occasion when he had been confronted in such a fashion. "I don't know you 'n' I'm willing to leave it that way."

"That sounds to me like you don't have the guts to stack up ag'in a *man* when he's ready,"

48

Birt declared. "Are you going to prove to all these fellers's're watching that I'm calling it wrong?"

Forcing himself to remember how his well-liked and respected boss had stated there must be no trouble in Child City, Bush made no reply. Young he might be, but he had learned to think before acting. Since he had never before seen his challenger, his every instinct warned there was something more than a dislike of Texans behind the way he had been insulted. He was aware that there had been attempts to cause trouble between the Wedge and the AW, or bring them into disrepute among the people of the town. However, he had believed that these attempts had been brought to an end by the killing of Eisteddfod and Jeremy Korbin. Unless, he suddenly realized, the incident was being provoked by a man who did not know there would be no pay because the man who gave them the instructions was dead.

Although he was not afraid and knew he had proved sufficiently competent with a gun to save himself from the man he had had to kill outside the saloon, Bush did not want to be put into a position where he would have to face a showdown with a stranger against whom he had no reason to feel animosity. He had had childish notions about achieving some kind of superiority by shooting another—provided doing so was unavoidable and happened in what could be considered a fair fight—but he had not enjoyed being the cause of another human being's death. Nobody had blamed him, since he had been compelled to do so in defense of his own life. Nevertheless, when the incident was over and the full extent of its gravity had sunk home, he had hoped the need to do so would never arise again.

Then another memory came to the youngster. Peaceful Gunn had faced a confrontation with a man determined to force a fight the first time Bush had come to the town. The youngster would never forget the way in which the situation was dealt with by the seemingly mournful and frightened Wedge hand.

Bush decided he must try similar methods, if only to avoid going against the orders regarding conduct given by his boss.

I WOULDN'T, WAS I YOU-ALL!

Giving what was intended to be a shrug of disdain, but without moving his hands in any way that could be construed as a threatening gesture by a man looking for an excuse to make a draw and shoot, Thorny Bush started to move as if turning away from John Birt. However, he kept watch on the other via the reflection in the mirror behind the counter. The moment he saw Birt glance toward the other three hard cases, who were still keeping watch on the other occupants of the barroom, he began to put his plan into action. Not, however, with either of the ivory-handled Colt Cavalry Model Peacemakers that rode butt forward for a cross-draw in the holsters of his gunbelt, in the way he had copied from one of his idols.

During the eleven days that had elapsed since he saw Peaceful Gunn successfully employ such tactics, whenever he had enough privacy, the young Texan had sought to develop a similar skill. He had been helped by inadvertently having allowed the only man he admired more than Stone Hart to see him doing so. Quite proficient in such a technique, Dusty Fog had given him valuable advice that had already greatly enhanced his ability, and he put the lessons he had learned into practice with speed and considerable efficiency.

Pivoting swiftly in the direction from which he had started to turn, Bush lashed his right leg upward. Rising between Birt's inadvertently parted thighs, the sharp toe of his boot arrived at the point where it would achieve the most satisfactory effect. Caught on that especially vulnerable portion of the masculine anatomy with considerable force, the young hard case let out a croaking gurgle of agony. With his hands clasping at the point of impact, his hat jerked from his head as he began to fold at the waist and his legs buckled in further response to the wave of most painful nausea that assailed him. Nor were his misfortunes at an end. To ensure Birt was rendered *hors de combat* and unable to take the matter further at that time, the young Texan interlocked both hands and raised them to crash down onto the back of Birt's neck.

Even as Birt was going down like a back-broken rabbit, Bush realized that his own problems were far from over. Considerably startled by the unexpected turn of events, Birt's companions swung in his direction, their hands going to the butts of their weapons. He knew he did not have a hope in hell of preventing them from completing their draws and gunning him down, as he felt sure had been the intention of his would-be assailant. It was something he had not taken into account, and he concluded that he could soon be suffering the consequences for having failed to do so.

"I wouldn't, was I you-all!"

The words, in a Texas drawl, were accompanied by the clicking of a revolver being brought to full cock. And although the comment had been made in what sounded like a gently caressing tenor tone, the three hard cases, looking around, decided it held a deadly threat to them.

Furthermore, menacing as the man they guessed the speaker to be struck them at that moment, the trio discovered that he was not alone.

Because of his upbringing as a fully trained member of the Pehnane Comanche Dog Soldier war lodge and the way he had lived ever since, the Ysabel Kid never completely relaxed the wary vigilance such an education had instilled. Therefore, although he had appeared completely at ease and babyishly innocent in the way that had caused Birt to suggest him as a likely candidate for the role of victim eventually given to Bush, he had continued to keep his surroundings under constant if surreptitious observation.

On entering the barroom of the Arizona State Saloon, his sole intention to have some relaxation while his two *amigos* were engaged upon the same pursuit with business matters to follow, the Kid had subjected the hard cases to a careful scrutiny as thorough as the one Stone Hart had carried out. Not only had he seen the four hard cases, but he had immediately recognized them for what they were. Therefore, using the mirror behind the counter as Bush had done to such good effect when preparing to deal with Birt, he had continued to keep an eye on them without letting this become apparent.

Noticing the interest being shown first in himself and then directed to the group of younger cowhands—and remembering how two more of the same kind had attempted to embarrass Mrs. April Eardle by revealing her former identity in what he believed had been an attempt to provoke hostility between her husband and the local population—the black-clad Texan had been suspicious when he saw the way they were approaching the bar. His thoughts had been confirmed by the way Birt had behaved. While amused and pleased by the way Bush coped with the situation, it being in accord with the instructions given by Stone Hart to the crew of the Wedge before they set out for town, the Kid had realized that Bush had failed to appreciate all the ramifications of what was happening and could therefore need help.

The black-clad Texan was ready to take action when the time came. And, being wise in such matters, before speaking he had made himself ready to deal with whatever might eventuate. But he knew this situation was unlike that outside Clitheroe's General Emporium; he knew his massive James Black bowie knife would not serve his needs, despite having been made to the same general dimensions as the one from the same maker that was wielded to such excellent effect by Colonel James Bowie on more than one occasion. Therefore, he had drawn and cocked the old Colt Dragoon revolver before making his seemingly gentle declaration.

Hearing what was said, Jamie Cann and the other two hard cases swung their gazes in the direction of the speaker. Of them all, only Harold Best had no need to look before knowing who had spoken. However, on making the discovery, Thomas Terry and their self-appointed leader quickly realized why their companion had given the warning when Birt had suggested the black-clad and naive-looking young Texan as the subject for their intentions. No longer did the Kid strike either of them as being a suitable victim. Instead, his appearance was that of a Comanche *tehnep*[†] waiting for the smallest excuse to go after a hated white-eye brother.

To eyes as well versed in such matters as were those of the three hard cases, everything about the posture of the Kid was one of instant readiness. The supposition was proven by the casual-seeming yet menacing way in which he had already drawn and cocked the old four-pound-one-ounce thumb-busting giant of a revolver that might be termed the grandfather of the Colt Peacemaker, now regarded by many as the greatest fighting handgun of the day. Its seven-and-a-half-inch-long round barrel might be dangling toward the floor, but it would swiftly be raised into alignment, ready to cut loose with

[†]Tehnep: *A fully trained and experienced warrior. As is the case with all the other Comanche terms given in the narrative, the spelling is phonetic and based on the definitive work about that nation:* THE COMANCHES, Lords of the South Plains, *by Ernest Wallace and E. Adamson Hoebel, University of Oklahoma Press.*

the .44-caliber loads in the cylinder should the need arise.

Having formed a similar appreciation of the situation, although none had gone as far as drawing a weapon, the group with whom the Kid had been speaking were formed in a rough half-circle around him. They might have empty hands, but the hard cases formed the impression that all were ready to participate should the need arise. In addition, every other cowhand in the room, recognizing Cann and the other two for what they were, was showing the animosity most of their kind had for hired guns. Indeed, even the group of soldiers at the table were displaying a dislike for the trio. Cann and his companions were professional fighting men who had had far more practice at handling weapons than the majority of cowhands had, but they knew they were far outnumbered and were sure to be rough-handled or worse should they attempt to take any kind of hostile action.

None of the trio wanted to let it be seen that they had backed water before the quietly spoken threat. Nor could any of them see a way by which they could avoid failing in whatever retaliatory action they elected to take. The black-dressed and deadly-looking Texan would be able to cut loose before any of them could complete a draw. His fame as a fighting man *par excellence* was based more on his expert use of the bowie knife sheathed at his left side or the Winchester Model 1873 "One of a Thousand" rifle he had won as first prize in a match against a number of his peers at the Cochise County Fair at Tombstone, although it was not to be seen. However, they concluded that he possessed sufficient skill with the old Colt to be able to take out at least one of them should the need arise. And although another of them might get him, none of them were likely to survive the attack that the cowhands to his immediate rear looked ready to launch and the rest around the room were certain to join.

Cann and his companions knew they had not the slightest hope of survival if gunplay started. But before the need arose for the trio to make a decision, the matter was taken from their hands!

"All right, now," said a quietly authoritative voice. "What's coming off in here?"

It was probably the first time in their misspent lives that Cann, Best, and Terry had found themselves almost relieved to be addressed by a peace officer.

But each of the trio realized that, while they might no longer be in danger of attack by the cowhands, they were still far from out of woods. Competent as he looked and they had heard he was, the man wearing the badge of county sheriff who was walking forward with a steady, determined stride was not coming alone to carry out an investigation into the incident.

None of the hard cases wondered how the peace officer had found out his presence was required, despite there having been no noise or other disturbance. What was more, even without needing to call for assistance from the occupants of the barroom, he was being given what looked like very capable support from the men who were fanning out just to his rear, each with an unrestricted line of fire if shooting should be called for.

On seeing the likelihood of trouble, the oldest of the saloon girls had left the group of cowhands from the Arrow P with whom she had been talking and hurried to the back room. Entering without the formality of knocking for once, she had told the assembled men what was about to take place. Turning from the bar, Sheriff Amos Reeves set off to do his duty as the senior peace officer in Spanish Grant County. Although his only deputy was not present, he was followed in rapid succession by Dusty Fog, Mark Counter, Stone Hart, Major Wilson Eardle, and Counselor Edward Sutherland. Individually they would have provided adequate support in whatever situation developed, but together they were a formidable force indeed. While the attorney could not claim to be a fighting man with anywhere near the stature of the others— although his Highland Scottish ancestors had been better than fair along those lines and he possessed a sturdy spirit—he had his authority as the region's justice of the peace to throw behind the sheriff.

Certainly Cann and his companions were in no doubt over what they were up against. Each one of the approaching party, even the short and chubby town-dweller, looked like a man to step aside from in time of trouble. That was even more so in the case of the Texan they had earlier dismissed. There was now something about him that stopped any of them from regarding him as small. Once again, even though he did not attempt in any way to usurp Reeves's position, the sheer strength of Dusty's personality gave him the appearance of being the biggest man present.

"Hell, my cousin there wasn't but looking to join in the fun those cowhands was having," Cann asserted, gesturing to where Birt lay motionless with his face in a pool of vomit. "That damned beef—cowhand jumped him afore he'd said more'n a couple of words."

"Well, now, Sheriff," the Kid drawled, having twirled away the Dragoon as soon as he heard Reeves speak. No longer did he seem charged with lethal menace; instead he looked as meek and mild as a pew full of choirboys. The tone of his voice was once again gentle and also respectful as he continued, "While I wouldn't want to call nobody a *liar,* that don't strike me as being the truthful true way I saw what come off."

"Cowhands allus stick together," Best pointed out before the black-dressed Texan could continue, speaking as if supplying information he believed the sheriff would not possess.

"I've heard tell of such afore today," Reeves replied dryly, Satisfied that he could do so in safety, he took his attention from the trio to look around the barroom for somebody who might be considered an impartial witness. "Which same's how saloon folks allus stand by their regular customers afore any of you tell me."

"Did you see what happened, Sergeant Zmijewski?" Eardle called, having recognized the noncom of the blue-uniformed party, although he had failed to do so, when they entered the saloon and made their way to the back room. Then a frosty grin came to his face as he glanced at the sleeves of the blue uniform shirt, and he went on, "Oh, so it's back to corporal *again,* I see. What was it this time?"

"Mistaken identification it *could* have been called, Major, sir," the stocky corporal replied with the voice of a well-educated man as he came to his feet and into a brace. He had been successful in concealing his slightly Mongoloid bronzed features when his former well liked and respected officer came into the saloon, since he had wanted to avoid letting his most recent reduction in rank be seen. "A bunch of muleskinners mistook me for a feller who needed to learn how to play poker."

"I can guess the rest," Eardle said dryly, yet with an underlying friendly amusement. "Unless these gentlemen think the ser—*corporal* and his troopers will stick together with the cowhands, perhaps he can say what happened, Sheriff?"

"How do *you* feel about it, mister?" Reeves inquired.

"Well—!" Cann began, without feeling any of the satisfaction he might otherwise have experienced over the implication that he was the leader of his party.

"I hope you're not going to imply my word isn't to be trusted," Corporal Antek Zmijewski said almost mildly, coming to his feet and marching with the gait of the cavalryman he had been for many years rather than just walking forward. "Because a man with a thirst like mine couldn't live on the pay of a buck private."

"Tell it, Ski," the sheriff requested.

"That knobhead lying there messing up the floor wasn't looking to join in any fun," Zmijewski concluded after describing what had taken place with complete accuracy and veracity. "And what he said wasn't put out in fun. Which the young Texan took him down as neat as I've ever seen. Did *you* have the teaching of him, Cap'n Fog?"

"Only in a small way, Corporal," Dusty replied, trying to remember where he had met the noncom and for once unable to decide. Then he went on with what he considered well-deserved praise, which gave Bush great pleasure. "Young Thorny's got natural talent without anybody needing to show him the way."

Hearing the name that had been supplied by the corporal, the suspicions that the three hard cases had formed with regards to the dusty-blond Texan were at last confirmed. Now they all knew that the man they had dismissed as insignificant was in reality the Rio Hondo gun wizard, Dusty Fog. The discovery did not lead to any lessening of the anxiety they were experiencing. It was apparent to even Best, who was the least intelligent of the quartet with the exception of Birt, that the task they had expected having no great difficulty carrying out was not going to be an easy matter. In fact, all three were beginning to mentally curse Taos Lightning Round for having got them into such a position.

"I goes along with Ski," the senior of the bartenders declared and, secure in his position as an unofficial leading member of the community—in fact, one of the most important leaders in the eyes of his customers—continued with a scathing stare at the trio of hard cases, "And I don't give a shit if anybody reckons I'm siding with them's regular' spend in here 'stead of just passing through and I reckon'll real soon be moving on."

"Are you bunch working around here?" Reeves asked, paying no attention to Birt, who was groaning his way back to a conscious and agony-filled state.

"Just passing through," Cann answered sullenly.

"Then I reckon it's time you *passed*," the sheriff said.

"We've not busting any laws!" Terry pointed out in as near a truculent fashion as he could muster against the coldly disapproving eyes that seemed to be picking him out as their subject. "You can't just up 'n' tell us to move on."

"I'll have to affirm that, according to the letter of the law, he has a *point*, Sheriff," Sutherland boomed in his most legalistic fashion. "They can't just be ordered to leave. You could have all the liber-rad softshells up to the Territorial Capital accusing you of violating their rights if you gave them the heave-ho."

"They'll get goddamned thirsty and hungry, comes to that should they stay," Angus McTavish declared in his broadest Scottish burr. He and the rest of the group who had gone into the back room on arrival had returned and formed a forbidding backup to the sheriff's party. "Because, much as it would pain my kind and generous heart to turn away business, they'll get no more service in here."

"Nor anywhere else," Amos Clitheroe asserted, the memory of how he had been treated by two hard cases in the employ of Eustace Edgar Eisteddfod still rankling. "We don't need their kind in Child City."

"There is one thing to give you the answer, Sheriff," Sutherland pontificated. "Under Article Seventeen Twenty-eight, Subparagraph Sixteen, Stroke Two-B of the Territorial Legislation, a

61

peace officer has the bounden right and duty to cause to vacate his bailiwick any person and his known associates who may be suspected of causing or possibly becoming involved in trouble or hostility therein." He paused as if wishing to make sure that the full majesty of the statement was being absorbed. Then he went on, "Now, I'm not saying any of these three gentlemen would do either, but their companion will doubtless be bearing a grudge against the young man responsible for his misfortunes. To prevent him from being further injured in an ill-advised attempt to seek revenge, which as good friends they will be expected to support, I must authorize you in my capacity of Justice of the Peace for Spanish Grant County to invoke the powers vested in you by the said Article to prevail on them to leave."

"You heard His Honor?" Reeves inquired. "Well, we're in no rush to see you gone. Anytime in the next half hour will do. Me and my deputies, Cap'n Fog, Mark Counter, 'n' the Ysabel Kid, will be around to make sure you've gone when the time's up."

"Haul Johnny onto his feet," Cann snarled at his companions. "We're getting out of here!"

"We'll just come along to see you do," the sheriff stated.

On returning with the three members of Ole Devil Hardin's floating outfit from watching the hard cases ride out of town, the sheriff went over to Sutherland and said in an admiring tone, "I never knew you're so well up in the Territorial Legislation, Counselor."

"I'm *not*," the attorney admitted with a grin. "Fact being, I just made the numbers and that

Article up. And now I'll take the glass of good Scotch whisky you're going to buy me for my legal services."

Before payment could be made, or the sheriff was able to say that he considered the legal services worth two drinks and a cigar—as he took great pleasure informing Sutherland later that he was intending to do—there was an interruption.

"Hey, Toby Canoga!" a freckle-faced red-haired youngster called, dashing through the front entrance. "Your Matilda's done had her a baby." Then, showing he clearly considered the next item of news he was to impart to be of vastly greater importance, he continued, "There's some freight wagons just come in to unload gear at the old *cantina,* and *Calamity Jane's* with 'em!"

"You *sure* of that, *amigo,*" Mark Counter asked in a worried tone.

"I certain sure am," the boy declared. "I heard one of the other drivers call her 'Calam' and no other woman could handle a bullwhip the way *she* was doing."

"Oh, Lord!" the blond giant groaned. "If we weren't in trouble before, we sure as sin's for sale in Cowtown are *now.* Fact being, I wonder just how *soon* that red-topped bundle of female perversity's going to stir some up?"

THAT'S NO WAY TO TREAT A LADY

To give credit where credit was due, the young person who had provoked the statement from Mark Counter at the Arizona State Saloon had not the slightest intention of getting involved in any kind of trouble.

Rather, the circumstances that arose were of the kind that had happened with such frequency during the eventful life of Miss Martha Jane Canary that she had acquired the nickname "Calamity."

In her early twenties, Calamity Jane presented a most attractive—albeit decidedly unconventional—picture. Five foot seven in height, beneath a dark blue United States Cavalry kepi perched at a jaunty angle on a mop of shortish and curly red hair, she had a face that was merry and comely rather than ravingly beautiful—tanned, sprinkled with freckles that added to rather than detracted from its charm, it had sparkling blue eyes, a slightly snub nose, and a mouth that looked made for laughing or kissing. However, as anybody who knew her would not hesitate to proclaim, she could cut loose with a hide-blistering flow of coarse profanity when a situation called for it.

That the redhead was a young woman endowed with a full and firm physique Junoesque in dimensions was shown all too plainly by her attire. A tightly rolled, multihued bandanna trailed its long ends over the well-filled bosom of a tartan shirt hugging her torso's contours like a second skin. The shirt's unfastened neck was open slightly lower than was decorous, and the top of a man's red flannel undershirt made an appearance across the gap. Like the garment tucked into its waistband, the Levi's pants gave the impression of having been bought a size too small and shrunk further during washing; they conformed almost perfectly to her well-rounded hips and buttocks. In the manner of cowhands and other male wearers west of the Mississippi River, the legs had the cuffs turned up about three inches to serve as a repository for nails and other small articles. Slanting down from her right hip, a well-designed gunbelt carried an ivory-handled Colt Model of 1851 Navy revolver—the bullets in its loops indicating one that had the Thuer conversion to accept metallic .36-caliber cartridges—butt forward in a holster tied to her right thigh by a pigging thong as an aid to ease of withdrawal. On the left side was a wide loop of leather through which was thrust the handle of a bullwhip, its long lash coiled for ease of carrying. As was the case with her well-known ability at plain, fancy, or inspired "cussing," those who could claim her acquaintance knew neither the gun nor the whip was a mere affectation.

Until the fates decreed otherwise, the curvaceous redhead was at peace with the world as she strolled away from her wagon after doing what she could for the team prior to the load being removed. Having carried out the delivery that she and the three other drivers employed by Cecil "Dobe" Killem had been told to make, she meant to do nothing more than ride the bedsprings out of the belly of her buckskin gelding—which she had led saddled and tied by its split-ended reins to the rear of the vehicle—while collecting some smoking material from a store in town. The route they had taken to arrive at the point to which they were directed by the men claiming ownership of the cargo was such that they had not come through the center of Child City, and she knew nothing of its facilities. Nevertheless, she felt certain she would find at least one of the establishments she needed. And if there should be a bathhouse available or the local hotel offered bathing facilities, she wanted to take a hot bath and change into clean clothes.

Before the redhead could liberate the buckskin, she saw a big dog loping along from across the range; she recognized it as the Chesapeake Bay retriever that served Margaret Hart so well. One of the reasons that Calamity had volunteered to help make the delivery, despite having taken a dislike to the pair who had hired Killem, was that she knew Spanish Grant County was where the Harts had come to make a new home for the Wedge. Although she had avoided the disturbing state of being compelled to don feminine attire and serve as a bridesmaid, which had happened to her on an earlier occasion, she had attended their wedding and even offered them her freight wagon if it could be of any service to them. Therefore, she was pleased to see the dog; she guessed it would be able to lead her to the Harts.

"Just take a look at *that,* Der'," said a masculine voice with a grating New England accent that Calamity had no difficulty identifying.

"I am, Steve," replied another speaker whose speech betrayed origins in Illinois and, once again, the redhead knew who he was. "Let's get old Buster 'n' have us some *fun.*"

Realizing what was meant and having no liking for it, the redhead swung around. She had no trouble locating the two men whose comments were causing her alarm and annoyance.

Derek Hatton was slightly more than medium

height and thickset, more fat than hard muscle. Even his mother could not truthfully claim he was good-looking; rather, he had unprepossessing features set in sullen lines suggestive of the cruelly vicious nature that the girl knew he possessed. He was dressed in the style of an Easterner, even though he wore a Colt Peacemaker in the tied-down holster of a Western gunbelt. On a couple of occasions he had shown off his ability at using it, but she—who considered herself something of a connoisseur where the subject was concerned—did not regard him as a threat. Certainly a number of her friends who were highly thought of in matters *pistolero* would not lose any sleep over the prospect of having to face him.

Some three inches taller than his partner and lean to the point of being gaunt, Steven Scott was not much of an improvement where looks were concerned. His attire was that of a successful gambler. He carried a Mervyn & Hulbert Model of 1876 Army Pocket revolver, with a three-and-five-sixteenths-of-an-inch round barrel and an ivory butt, thrust into the left side of the black silk sash about his middle so it could be drawn by reaching across with his right hand. Although Calamity had never seen a demonstration, he had often boasted of his skill at drawing fast and shooting with accuracy.

Nothing that had happened during the journey since the cargo was picked up at Prescott had caused Calamity to revise the less-than-flattering opinion she had formed of the pair on first meeting them. They were loudmouthed bullies who took delight in causing pain to be inflicted on animals, or humiliating men they regarded as being safe to antagonize. It had taken the use of some very strong language and a demonstration of how effectively she could handle her long-lashed bullwhip and Navy Colt to convince them that she was to be treated just like the male drivers. What was more, her fellow workers had stated their support for her and warned that any further complaints would see the cargo dumped no matter where it took place. Despite having along ten burly men of the kind frequently seen in saloons of the less honest and savory variety, so firm a stance was taken by the salty handlers of the wagons—who all clearly meant to carry out the threat and were obviously competent enough to do so— that the pair had taken the warning to heart and there were no further incidents.

One of the many things that had caused the animosity the redhead felt toward Hatton and Scott was what they considered to be a hilarious sport. Hatton had brought along a powerful fair-sized dog that was an admixture of the English bull terrier and other breeds of the kind that would eventually develop into the notorious American pit bull. Throughout the journey, except when prevented by Calamity and the drivers, they had delighted in turning the vicious brute loose upon other dogs that came their way and watching the resultant activity, which was almost always a slaughter. They had evidently decided that, having arrived at their destination, they could indulge in their so-called sport again without needing to fear any consequences.

"Hold it, you pair!" Calamity yelled. When she raised her voice, her fellow drivers always claimed it could be heard for a good country mile even with a Texas blue-norther gale blowing into her face. "What the hell do you reckon you're going to do?"

"Have us some *fun*," Hatton claimed, glancing around to make sure all the male drivers were busy elsewhere.

"Not with *that* dog," the redhead stated flatly. "He's Rollo, and acts as eyes for Margaret Hart on account of she's blind."

"It's just another cur, to me," Scott declared. "How about you, Der'?"

"That's how I see it," the New Englander confirmed. "And old Buster hasn't had him a good workout for days."

"And he's *not* going to get one today," Calamity asserted, standing with feet spread apart and hands on hips in a way anybody who knew her well recognized as a position of readiness. "Ole Rollo there's too damned important to a friend of mine for you to use him in your lousy games."

"Do you reckon you can stop us?" Derek challenged, a remembrance of having a cigar disintegrated in his face by the lash of the bullwhip still rankling.

"Do you reckon I can't?" the redhead countered tensely, ready to take whatever kind of action was necessary.

"I'll not stand still for you fooling with that goddamned whip again!" Scott warned in an ugly and menacing tone.

"Mister," Calamity answered. "Should I need it, I won't be *fooling* this time."

"You talk real big for a woman," Hatton snarled. "Or do you reckon you being one'll stop us from handing you your needings if we have to?"

"Nope," the redhead replied. "Fact being, I reckon the both of you'd sooner mishandle a woman than a man, figuring it'd be *safer.*"

"Go turn Buster loose, Der'!" Scott snapped, his right hand pointing toward the butt of the Mervyn & Hulbert. "She's just a loudmouthed lobby-lizzie in men's clothes, and I'm quick sick of taking the bullshit she's been handing out all the way here."

Watching the two men, Calamity knew that she was facing a showdown. Although not afraid, she realized that she was in a dangerous position. Her every instinct warned that if push came to shove, Hatton would be ready to help out Scott instead of doing as he was told. She might not have any great respect for either's ability at handling a gun in a one-on-one showdown, but she knew the pair of them would prove more than she could handle. However, having taken grave exception to being referred to as a lobby-lizzie—a prostitute—her stubborn pride, born of a self-reliant nature that allowed her to stand on her own feet in any kind of situation, refused to allow her to take the sensible course of calling to her companions for help.

"Was I asked," said a voice with a gentle-sounding Texas drawl that sounded like the sweetest music to the girl's ears, "I'd say that's no way to treat a lady—if you'll forgive me for calling you that, Calam."

Because Mark Counter had had to go with Dusty Fog into the back room at the saloon to attend to some business matters, the Ysabel Kid had considered it incumbent upon himself— as the only available member of Ole Devil Hardin's floating outfit—to go greet a friend with whom they had all spent happy hours and not a few dangerous moments. He had also wanted to collect his Winchester rifle, which he had left leaning by the front door of Clitheroe's General Emporium after dealing with the two hard cases set upon revealing the secret of April Eardle's past. He had been told by the wife of the owner that it had been placed behind the counter for safekeeping, but he never felt entirely at ease when it was not someplace where it could be easily reached should its special services be needed.

On hearing what the black-dressed Texan wanted to do, Amos Clitheroe had not hesitated before accompanying him to the store and returning the weapon. With this achieved, the Kid had set off to where the storekeeper told him the deserted *cantina* was located. While approaching, he had seen and heard enough to indicate that his big blond *amigo* had been right in claiming that Calamity would soon be hip-deep in some kind of trouble. He had also concluded that she was going to need a mite of help with the situation in which she had become involved. Therefore, he had come upon the scene without having been detected by any of the participants until he spoke.

"I'll forgive you just this once, Lon," Calamity declared, trying not to let her sense of relief show, especially to a good friend who knew her as well as he did. "Only, don't you go making a habit of calling me no *lady*."

While the redhead was speaking, Hatton and Scott looked at the man who had intervened, wishing that all their men were not fully occupied in storing the equipment and stock of liquor from the wagons. First they took in the sight of the black-clad and very young-looking figure standing in an attitude of apparently unconcerned ease. Next they gave a quick glance at the armament he was wearing around his waist. However, their main attention was given to the magnificent Winchester Model of 1873 rifle that he was grasping by the wrist of its butt in his right hand, the barrel resting on his shoulder so the muzzle was pointing away from them. Although the weapon was more readily available than either his revolver or bowie knife, which they took as nothing more than ostentatious adornments to convey a nonexistent maturity and toughness, neither felt in any way disturbed or threatened by his presence.

"What's it all about, Calam?" the Kid inquired, walking forward with a leisurely stride that reminded the redhead of the gait employed by cougar stalking its prey.

"These pair've got them a real *mean* dawg they like to sic onto others for what they call fun," Calamity explained. "Only, it's closer to setting a catamount onto a sheep most times. Right now, they've concluded to turn that mean bastard onto Margaret Hart's Rollo, if you know who I'm talking about."

"I *do,* seeing as how Dusty, Mark, 'n' me come in with her 'n' Stone just now," the black-dressed Texan confirmed, and suddenly he no longer looked young or harmless. Instead, his whole being became charged with the cold and deadly threat of his Pehnane Comanche heritage. "Do you pair still have a mind to do it?"

"We do!" Hatton claimed. His duties as owner of the saloon that he and Scott had come to

72

start in the cantina did not require him to be susceptible to atmosphere or to be able to assess another person's character.

"Has Calam told you what Rollo's used for?" the Kid asked.

"That's none of our worry," the New Englander declared, although he was beginning to believe it would have been better for him to have kept his mouth shut.

"She tell you how important he is for helping Mrs. Hart to get along, her being blind?" the Kid queried with no change in his tone.

"That's her lookout, not our'n," Hatton stated. "Buster needs a workout, and we aim to see he gets it."

"Then do it, if you're so set," the Kid said quietly, glancing to where the Chesapeake Bay retriever was still in view. "Only, as soon as that dawg of your'n makes a move towards Rollo, I'm going to blow its head off with my first bullet."

"First bullet," Hatton repeated in a puzzled tone.

"The next two'll be for you pair, seeing as how it'll be 'cause of you your dawg got made wolf bait," the black-dressed Texan explained, still without bringing the Winchester into a position of greater readiness. "So it all comes down to *you.* Try to have your dawg-fight if you're still so inclined, or get on with whatever chores you'd be better off doing than taking what'll come to you."

There—the two men had the situation laid out for them as plain as they could want.

On the face of it, the solution should have been simple. Hatton and Scott thought they were very competent in handling their revolvers. Even counting the girl as a factor, which they did not for a moment doubt she would prove to be, they would still be going up against a single opponent each. However, there were disturbing factors to take into account. Not the least of these was the change that had come over the Texan whom they had at first thought to be no more than a dressed-up youngster trying to impress the redhead. Now, while his posture was still very much the same, his whole demeanor had changed; he conveyed a very dangerous competence mixed with Indian menace.

Suddenly neither Hatton nor Scott wanted to take the matter any further.

The only thing that was stopping either of the pair from making their feeling known was a desire to avoid letting it be seen that they lacked the guts to take up the challenge that had been thrown their way.

"Well, you pair of knobheads," Calamity said, impatient as always, when almost a minute had gone by without anybody speaking. "What's it going to be?"

"That damned dawg's gone now, Der'," Scott said, seeing a way out of the predicament and hoping his companion—at whom he had not glanced since the conversation started—would have enough sense to follow his lead instead of prodding their antagonists further. "So there's no point in turning Buster loose."

"And there'd better not be where Rollo's concerned, *hombres*," the Kid warned, knowing the affair was at an end but seeking to establish one point beyond all doubt. "Because, if he gets into fuss with that dawg of your'n, I'll be around to ask you the why-all of it— and I won't be coming friendly."

"We'll keep it in mind," Scott promised. "Come on, Der'. Let's go see how the fellers're getting on with the work."

"Yeah," Hatton agreed, his legs feeling weak under him as he contemplated how close he had come to getting killed. All he wanted to do was get away from the savagely threatening black-clad figure with the face that had suddenly taken on the appearance of an Indian brave, like the one in the painting of the Custer massacre that was to go behind the bar in the *cantina*. "We've got plenty that needs us on hand to make sure it gets done."

"Mark was right, Calam," the Kid drawled, watching the two men walk away at a faster-than-usual gait. "He allowed you'd soon enough find trouble now you've hit town."

The description of Mark Counter and her rescuer given by Miss Martha Jane Canary in response was blunt and profane.

I WANT HER OUT OF TOWN

"I'd say you handled things just right, Kid, although I'm not sorry it wound up without shooting," Sheriff Amon Reeves said after having been told about the incident near the old cantina. "I reckon I'll go around and have a talk to those two jaspers and let them know there'd better not be any dawgs hereabouts getting chawed up by their'n."

"I'll come with you, if you'll wait until I've

finished here," Counselor Edward Sutherland offered. "When I've greeted them in my capacity of Justice of the Peace for Spanish Grant County, I'll tell them that the liber-rad softshells at Prescott have brought in an ordinance against running cock- and dogfights. I heard tell they tried to get something like that on the books, and they might even have succeeded in doing so. At least, there's a good chance our visitors won't know whether they have or not."

"Complete with its Article name and number on the Legislation Statute books?" Dusty Fog guessed with a grin.

"Of course," the attorney agreed. "And now, gentlemen, to business."

By the time the Ysabel Kid had returned from his fortuitous visit to Calamity Jane, the birth of Matilda and Toby Canoga's son—whose weight had increased from the actual eight pounds until it had become necessary to hint to the proud father that sixteen was just a trifle unbelievable—had been given enthusiastic congratulations by everybody in the Arizona State Saloon. Leaving the rest of the crowd to continue the festivities—except Canoga, who had headed for the Sutherland house at something close to a run—the attorney, saying his home would be no fit place for men after what had happened there, had brought the interested parties into Angus McTavish's private office for the meeting they had come to Child City to carry out. They were Stone Hart, Major Wilson Eardle, Dusty Fog, and Mark Counter, with the sheriff asked to join them so the events of the day could be discussed officially.

The first item on the agenda had been the

two attempts by obvious hired guns to make trouble. The general consensus of opinion had been that both groups had been hired by the late Eustace Edgar Eisteddfod. Since none of them had been seen around the town, or at the old building where the rest were located and the survivors sent packing by the sheriff, it was also concluded that they were carrying out instructions without having become aware that the man who issued them was dead. If the past was any guide—Eisteddfod had sought to avoid letting it be suspected that he was responsible for the various incidents that were intended to provoke hostility between the two ranches and stir up animosity for the newly arrived owner of the Wedge ranch—it was a distinct possibility that the latest batch of troublemakers had been hired by proxy in some way and were told to do their work without making contact with him.

Accepting that the conclusions could explain the behavior of the pair and later the quartet of hard cases, and knowing that the rest of the meeting was on matters of business between the two ranchers and the attorney—with the two members of General Ole Devil Hardin's floating outfit invited to participate—Reeves had been on the point of taking his departure. Before he could do so, the Kid had arrived with the news about the incident at the old cantina. Hearing of what had been averted by the black-dressed Texan's intervention, the sheriff decided he had an even more pressing matter to attend to. He had not been surprised to receive an offer of assistance from Sutherland, which could pass as legal support for what he meant to do. It was not the first time in their acquaintance that Sutherland had willingly served in a similar capacity.

"I reckon we can hold off until you've 'tended to your legal duties, Ed," Stone Hart offered, and Eardle nodded his concurrence. "It will leave us to go have our talks with the banker, Wils."

"That it will," the owner of the AW ranch agreed. The visit to the Cattlemen's Bank had been an important reason for the visit to Child City. "I haven't seen anything of him."

"I'd say he's seen *you*," Sutherland remarked dryly. "Only, being the kind he is—or Mrs. Bank makes him be—he's standing on his dignity and waiting for *you* to make the first move."

"Not the sociable kind, huh?" Stone guessed, taking notice of the emphasis put on the name given to the woman he deduced was the wife of the banker.

"I don't think he would be, even if Mrs. Bank would let him," the attorney assessed. "The only person he ever showed any signs of being will-ing to associate with outside banking hours was Eisteddfod, and they seemed as alike as two peas in a pod in the way they talked and acted."

"That's not what you'd expect from a banker," Dusty drawled.

"Maybe not," Sutherland replied. "But he's the only game in the county and probably doesn't think he needs to go to the expense some of us are *forced* into because folks have nowhere else to go unless they want to take a long ride one way or another."

"I've heard you're the only game in town on the law-wrangling side, Counselor," Mark commented. He had come to know the attorney well enough to feel sure his words would not cause offense.

"It doesn't give me any satisfaction," Sutherland claimed, so soberly he might have conceded that the remark was accurate. "Only, I still get a muckle amount of expenses forced on me by my Flora's social position in the community."

"I hate it when he starts talking broad Scotch," Reeves informed the Texans in an equally somber fashion, aware that the attorney—who was a good friend and hunting partner as well a supportive ally in all matters legal—invariably responded to anybody who used the word "Scotch" when referring to his race. "It means he's looking for either a free drink or cigar to be offered out of sympathy."

"That statement is so close to being libelous that it could be actionable," the attorney warned in his best court-of-law manner. "Which, I would remind you, I'd be sat on the bench should it be brought. On the rare occasions when I am in receipt of a wee dram or a smokie, it is for giving of my free time for a legal consultation. And, when you're ordering my justified fee for the one I've just given, I'll have a *Scottish*."

"You can't win with him," Reeves informed the other men around the desk in a resigned fashion. "It all depends which side he's on how he feels about a point of law and what side he takes."

"You Yankees were always sneaky," Stone drawled, confident that the remark would not be regarded by Eardle and the local men as anything more than a joke.

"That's why we won the late conflict of interests," the owner of the AW claimed, equally convinced the Texans—who had all supported the Confederate cause during the War Between the States—would not take offense. "Will my wife have met Mrs. Bank?"

"I wouldn't say that's likely," Reeves estimated. "She's never been the one for socializing and isn't even a member of the Child City Civic Betterment League."

"Which is a blessing," the attorney declared with a fervency that almost seemed genuine. "It's one less expense for me at their gatherings, although I don't doubt I'll have three more by now."

"Let's go see the banker, shall we, Stone?" Eardle suggested. "I can't bear to watch a grown man cry, even if he is a law-wrangler."

"Or me," the boss of the Wedge ranch agreed. "Anyways, before you start to sobbing out your generous li'l ole heart, Counselor, Wils and I are going to have the roundup started while we're over to the Land Office in Prescott to put in bids for Eisteddfod's spread and the Arrow P. Steve Baird and Ed Leshlin say they'll come in with us, since they're still staying on as *segundos* of the spreads, unless it's against the law for them to take so much on themselves with both owners dead."

"I don't see that there would be objections to it, even should there be heirs to the properties that we haven't heard from yet, it will be as much to their benefit as yours," Sutherland replied, and despite knowing that this subject was of considerable importance, went on,

"Which, I must point out, is a *considered* legal opinion."

"And worth a whole drink of good *Scottish*," Eardle stated, just as aware as the sheriff had been about the different connotations of the two words. "With a cigar thrown in to boot, provided you'll go halves with the cost, Stone."

"I'll be damned if it's not catching, Amon," the Texan rancher told the sheriff in tones of resignation, looking in a noticeably pointed fashion from his Yankee counterpart to the attorney before going on more seriously. "Anyways, we'll have the roundup started like we planned. Wils and I figure we'll have Dusty as roundup captain, with Mark as his straw boss, and the *segundos* all agreed it'll be for the best."

"So do I," Sutherland declared. He knew that acting as roundup captain was far from being a sinecure when several ranches were involved. It called for a man with a sufficiently powerful personality, a man known for having considerable ability in all aspects of the cattle-raising business, to command the number of cowhands involved and prevent any clashes of interests brought about by each's feelings of loyalty to his spread. He felt sure that the *big* dusty-blond Texan was ideally suited for the duty and had handled it before. "If there is any way I can be of assistance, Captain Fog, don't hesitate to let me know."

"Only if my bosses put down in writing they'll cover whatever consultation fees that come up," Dusty answered cheerfully. "From what I've heard, you even charge them should somebody say, 'Good morning, isn't it a nice day?'"

"That's just a vicious rumor started by folks who're too parsimonious to pay their legal dues," the attorney said, wondering how he had ever thought of the Texan as small and insignificant. "And, as it is patently obvious I'm among such now, in my official albeit *unpaid* capacity of Justice of the Peace for Spanish Grant County, I propose we go and interview the new arrivals in our fair city, Sheriff."

"You wouldn't want to deputize me for a spell, would you, Amon?" Mark inquired before the suggestion could be acted upon. "*Unpaid,* of course, Mr. Justice of the Peace for Spanish Grant County."

"It would have to be unpaid, as we've already got one deputy around who doesn't earn all the money we good taxpaying citizens of the county have to fork out for his wages," Sutherland said. "So why do you want for the sheriff to take you on?"

"So I can go run that blasted Calamity Jane out of town," the blond giant replied. "Because, like I said and was soon enough proved, if we didn't have trouble before she got here, we'll sure as sin's for sale in Cowtown get more of it now she's here."

"Do you reckon those two fellers might take after her, looking for evens, Mark?" the sheriff asked.

"If they should," the blond giant answered with a broad grin, "what I've good cause to know of her, my sympathies would all be with *them*. Not only is that red-topped bundle of perversity full capable of taking care of herself, I'd sooner tangle with a winter-starved Texas flatheaded grizzly—which everybody know is the biggest, heaviest and meanest of all its kind— than those fellers who're with her if they take the notion she's being picked on and needs helping. No, sir, the only reason I want her out of town is that things're like' to be a whole heap more peaceable that way."

"Good afternoon, gentlemen," Robin C. Harman said with far less warmth than might have been expected where prospective clients were concerned. Harman was generally believed around Child City to be the owner of the Cattlemen's Bank only as far as his wife, Harriet, would permit. "Can I be of service in some way to you?"

"You can, I should imagine," Major Wilson Eardle replied dryly, thinking back to the attorney's remark about the bank being the only game of its kind in town and concluding that there was justification for the description. He wondered whether the man he was addressing believed that he and his companion had arrived hoping to obtain loans, and he decided to set the matter right. "We've both come to make a deposit."

The meeting in Angus McTavish's private office at the Arizona State Saloon had concluded with Sheriff Amon Reeves declining to appoint Mark Counter as even an unpaid temporary deputy on the grounds that to do so might lead to an abuse of his authority—justifiable though it might be—in ordering a visitor to get out of town. While the peace officer and Counselor Edward Sutherland set out to interview the new arrivals at the cantina, the three members of the Ole Devil Hardin's floating outfit went to join the celebrations in the barroom.

Taking up the money and other items that they had brought with them from their homes, the two ranchers had left the saloon to carry out their business at the bank. They had arranged to meet outside the premises on reaching the town, but had carried out their intention of seeing their crews off in a celebration prior to the commencement of the roundup, which would establish as near as humanly possible exactly how many head of cattle each owned. The period that had elapsed since the death of Eustace Edgar Eisteddfod brought a cessation to the troubles that had threatened the peace of the County had been spent by Stone Hart and his crew getting to know what was now their home range. Hart and his men had driven in all the animals they found bearing the C Over M brand used by his late uncle to have a vent applied and his own mark of ownership substituted.

Passing through the barroom, Eardle had delayed long enough to ask whether Corporal Antek Zmijewski would be at liberty to wait and join him in a drink to talk over old campaigns. On being assured that the soldiers were away from Fort Mescalero on an official pass, he told the noncom to have a round of drinks for them put on his account. Then, to the amusement of Stone—who was waiting close enough to hear what was being said—he warned that there would be no sending one of the troopers to order a whiskey and five beers, then going over and saying, "And I'll take the same myself." Going by the grin that had come to Zmijewski's leathery face, the boss of the Wedge spread concluded that the ruse had been carried out before.

With that matter attended to, the two ranchers had carried on with their business affairs. They had been admitted to Harman's office after being greeted less than enthusiastically by a lean and miserable-looking, long-haired young man who did not look comfortable in a badly fitting blue uniform—resembling those worn by police officers in Eastern cities—with a revolver in the holster from which they assessed it would be difficult to draw in an emergency. On being told why they had come, saying there was no teller on duty, he had gone through the door inscribed with ROBIN C. HARMAN, president, private and returned after a few seconds to say they could enter. Neither had been impressed by the appearance of the outer office or the man who was obviously employed as its guard. Nor did they find the office they entered to be any more grand.

"Very well," said the banker, whose second given name was Cook. He was a slim man of medium height, with a weak face not made any better-looking by an untidy growth of whiskers. Although his clothing was of good quality, it was more untidy than one might have expected from a person in his position. "As Cuthb—my guard will have told you, my teller isn't here right now."

"He's celebrating just become the father of a boy that'd got up to a full *twenty-three* pounds weight, which'd be a mite big even for a Texan, when we saw him last," Stone drawled, wondering whether he had ever met a man to whom

85

he took such an instant dislike as he did the banker. Deciding that the other was of the same kind as the bunch of particularly obnoxious young Easterners whom circumstances had compelled him to take along on the most unusual trail drive he had ever made, he saw no reason to change his feelings. "So we told him that he needn't stop the little feller growing just for us, as we figured you'd be here to 'tend to things for us."

"I'm sure I can," Harman conceded in a tone closer to grudging than obliging. He looked in turn at the large buckskin sacks each of his visitors was carrying. "So you both wish to make deposits?"

"Figured we might as well, seeing as how we'll both be around for a fair spell to come and don't have anything near as strong as your place'll be out to the ranches," Stone agreed. He wondered what had caused the brief play of emotion to cross the face of the banker.

"Very well," Harman said. "I'll deal with it myself."

Despite his aura of indifference, it was obvious to the ranchers that the banker was impressed by the sum of money and the value of the bank draft Stone placed before him. He was even more impressed when, after having concluded the formalities required to make the owner of the Wedge spread a depositor in the establishment, he saw the even larger sums that Eardle placed before him. What was more, saying that his wife figured she would not be needing it until they went someplace calling for its use, he added a small pile of jewelry to the rest of his property and asked for them to be stored in a personal safe-deposit box if one was available. Harman admitted in a snuffy voice that such facilities were available, then stared at the document from an insurance company well known nationwide which indicated that the items were of considerable worth.

"I won't take it amiss if you want to have them valued independently," Eardle stated as the banker looked from the jewelry to him and back again.

"There isn't any need for that," Harman replied, aware that there was nobody in the town outside the bank sufficiently qualified to carry out the valuation. He did not mention that he considered himself competent to carry out the examination, having worked in the jewelry trade before marrying his wife. Waving a flaccid hand toward what was obviously the door of a sturdily constructed vault, he went on, "You can put them into the box in there and rest assured they and all your other deposits will be perfectly safe in our care."

I DON'T LIKE COINCIDENCES

"I'll get back as soon as I can, honey," Stone Hart told his wife as they stood on the porch of what was now their home shortly after sunrise on the day after the eventful visit to Child City. Taking her into his arms, he went on, "And I'm going to miss you all the time I'm gone."

"Why can't you be romantic like the newlyweds, Wils?" April Eardle inquired, although her husband was treating her in the same fashion.

"I warned you from the start that I wasn't the romantic kind," Major Wilson Eardle replied. He and his wife had accepted the offer from the Harts that they stay for the night at the Wedge ranch house, despite having been warned that the guest room was on the small side. What was more, despite the comment he had made, they had spent a most enjoyable time in the somewhat confined dimensions of the bed. "And I think I proved it last night."

"Then who was I in bed with?" the gorgeous blonde asked so quietly that only the exceptionally keen ears of Margaret Hart heard the words, and she had other things on her mind at that moment to take any notice of what was being said.

"If you think that was something," the owner of the AW ranch stated, equally sotto voce, "just you wait until I get back. I'm going to eat plenty of rye bread both ways."

"That sounds like a promise, soldier boy," April commented, thinking with pleasure of how her husband had thawed out since meeting and making friends with the Texans. He had never been frigid, or an unsatisfactory lover, but he had changed in other ways that she considered to be beneficial. "And I'm going to hold you to it. Do you have any messages if Claude de Tornay comes for a visit while you're gone?"

"Yes," Eardle said in a mock grim fashion, since he had discovered from Corporal Antek Zmijewski that the commanding officer of Fort Mescalero was an old friend throughout much of their military career. "If he starts exerting his French charm, tell him I haven't forgotten why we called him 'Fancy Pants' at West Point."

"If he starts exerting his French charm, or any other kind," the blonde declared, "I'll kick him somewhere 'tween neck and knee the way I learned in the days before you saved me from a life of sin."

"I was damned angry when those two sons of bitches started to tell who and what you'd been," Eardle growled.

"You don't need to be," April assured her obviously still-incensed husband. He had always been touchy about any reference to the days when she was employed as an entertainer in saloons. And although the characterization was one she often employed while speaking of those days when they were alone, and occasionally in the company of people whom she trusted, she had never lived what might accurately be termed a life of sin. "I've never done anything I'm ashamed to own up to. Anyways, the way it turned out because of Mark and the Kid and the way all of you stood up for me, everybody knows now. What's more, I'm in so good with the womenfolks around Child City who count that they've asked me to help organize a show to raise money for a new roof on the church."

"I can just imagine some of them doing those high-kicking dances you used to teach the girls," the rancher said with a grin. "Anyway, dear, I can see Captain Fog giving us a 'Why don't you bunch finish off and light a shuck so I can get some work done' look. The U.S. Cavalry lost a hell of a good soldier when we didn't try to talk him into staying on instead of going back to Texas after the war ended."

"It lost one when I got *you*," the blonde asserted. "Give me a kiss and head off before I grow all maudlin and woman."

"We'd best head 'em up and move 'em out before Dusty swells up and bursts with impatience, honey," Stone was saying at the same moment. "Anyways, the sooner we get started, the sooner I'll be coming back."

"Eat some rye bread all the way there and back," Margaret suggested as she blushed. She had not been so totally absorbed in preparing for her husband's departure that she had failed to take in the reference made by Eardle.

"Huh?" Stone said in genuine puzzlement.

"I'll tell you when you get back," Margaret promised. "Now give me a kiss and head out before you have me joining April in some blubbering."

"Mark!" Dusty Fog barked while the almost identical requests were being carried out with gusto by the ranchers. "I didn't know it's April the twenty-first."

"It isn't," the blond giant replied, knowing what was coming.

"Nor even the Fourth of July?"

"Not that neither."

"Well, it just *can't* be Christmas, can it?"

"If it is," Mark Counter answered, "neither you nor Lon've bought me a present."

"Then why're all the hands *loafing* around here when there's work to be done?" the small Texan demanded in a tone his big *amigo* knew so well. "I had me just the teensiest notion they was supposed to be out on the range earning their pay."

"We're just off," Mark stated, and lifted his

voice in a bellow. "Let's get some leather 'tween our knees and ride!"

"Blast it all ways!" Rusty Willis muttered to his wife. They were standing together a short distance along the porch from the other two couples and engaged in similar talk and behavior. In addition to his tight-rolled bandanna, he had suspended around his neck a stiff leather board about six inches square in which had been burned the Wedge brand. Known as a "blab-board," it indicated that he was appointed as the "rep" for his outfit and would be responsible for ensuring that all the cattle belonging to it were kept clear of the rest, gathered and ready to be pushed on to home terrain. "I've got to head off now."

"*Good!*" the curvaceous ash-blonde replied with what appeared to be satisfaction, despite feeling pride that her husband was required to fill such an important position. "April's going to show me how to do some fancy high-kicking dance so I can help her teach it to the girls of the Betterment League for our show, and we don't want any of you menfolks hanging around while we're at it."

Even before Mark had completed the order, the cowhands, having noticed how the small Texan who was to be the roundup captain was eyeing them with none of the friendship exhibited at the Arizona State Saloon the previous day, were heading for the horses that were standing saddled and ready for use. They had been up long enough before sunrise to eat the meal prepared by Chow Willicka and his assistant, then collected the animals upon which they meant to start the day. While collecting his selection, Rusty remarked to Thorny Bush—who was similarly engaged—that Dusty must be getting all gentled down and kindhearted since being married, letting them spend so long without being found any work to do. Having heard the older Wedge hands tell of how the crew of the OD Connected ranch felt on the subject, the youngster stated that any change would have to be an improvement as, according to all accounts, he could not possibly have grown any meaner.

The selection of the members from each crew to work the roundup was different from what would have been the case in normal conditions. Even where the Wedge and AW spreads were concerned, in the light of the speculation aroused by the previous day's events it had been deemed prudent to ensure that each property's main buildings were adequately protected. Therefore, at Dusty's instigation, older members of the crews—enough to ensure security and perform the never-ending small chores that needed to be done—were assigned to the task. In every case the foreman would be in charge of those who were to stay behind.

There had been no objections to the arrangement. In fact, Jimmy Conlin, Steve Baird, and Ed Leshlin—respectively of the AW, Vertical Triple E, and the Arrow P—each said they felt it was a wise choice and that only good could accrue from the younger members of the crew working under two acknowledged masters of the trade like Dusty and Mark. Speaking in his capacity as *segundo* of the Wedge and a friend of long standing, Waggles Harrison had claimed that those who worked the roundup were going to decide that the devils they knew—himself and the other three—were preferable to that dusty-blond hell-twister from Rio Hondo County and his golden-blond giant straw boss who could be counted on to have adopted similar ways. After all, the four of them expected the crew to work only twenty-three hours a day and were willing to give Sunday afternoon off for churchgoing, but the two products of Ole Devil's floating outfit would expect a full twenty-five *per diem* and *eight* days a week, although he had heard they did not object if anybody wanted to have spiritual comfort on the Lord's day, provided it was taken quickly while riding along.

"Lon, Kiowa," Dusty called. "Hold it up a spell, will you, please?"

"Which means how he's got things brewing is *worse'n* riding roundup for us," the Ysabel Kid informed the other man addressed in a voice pitched just loud enough for the small Texan to be able to hear. Then, speaking louder and putting a mock ingratiating grin on his face, he continued, "Yes sir, Cap'n Fog, *sir,* was there something?"

"Why, sure, there just might be at that," Dusty answered, glancing to where the two ranchers were mounting the horses already fetched for them by Tarbrush, the lanky and always cheerful young Negro who had ridden as nighthawk for the Wedge on the trail drive from Texas to their new home. Now, as young Vincent Stretch had been elevated from the position of wrangler, which he held on the way to Spanish Grant County, Tarbrush—complaining that all the daylight might prove bad for his eyes—had assumed the work of looking after the remuda horses that were not being used. He was also leading a packhorse loaded with what their wives had decided they would need to make the correct impression for the visit to the office of the land agent in Prescott. "Fact being, there're a couple of shovels in the barn that need their blister ends riding."

"I don't even *know* this here blasted Pehnane slit-eye, Cap'n Fog, sir, much less 'sociate with the likes of him," Kiowa Cotton claimed with much the same kind of false humbleness the black-dressed Texan had used. He matched the Kid in height and had a similarly lean build, and his face was even more indicative of mixed ancestry. However, there was nothing suggestive of youthful innocence about his dark brown hawklike features. Instead, he gave the impression of being coldly efficient and deadly, which he in fact was when circumstances required these traits. Very competent at all aspects of scouting duties, he was another member of the OD Connected ranch's floating outfit, and had been sent by Ole Devil Hardin to serve Stone in that capacity during the trail drive to Spanish Grant County because the man who usually did so, Johnny Raybold, had had to go to New York on urgent family business.

"Which a medicine man I bribed with wampum once said I was some too feeble to ride the blister end of a shovel."

"The weakest thing about both of you is your *heads*," the small Texan growled. "Stay put while I have a word with the ladies."

"I thought you'd be off bullying the rest of those worthless vagabonds, Dusty," April remarked as the small Texan walked toward the porch.

"And I will be once we've had us a little talk," Dusty replied.

"That sounds ominous," the blonde stated. She had come to know *all* the three most prominent members of Ole Devil's floating outfit during the period following her making their acquaintance.

"It's something to do with Wils and Stone," Margaret went on. "Isn't it, Dusty?"

"Well, now you come to mention it," the small Texan replied with a wry grin, "I'll have to come on out all truthful truly and say, 'Yes, it is.' "

"I just *knew* there was something gnawing at you all the way back home last night," the blind woman declared with certainty. "It showed in the way you were only half listening to everything that was being said to you—and having the Kid riding a long circle around us."

"Calf rope," Dusty drawled, raising his hands in a gesture of surrender. Glancing around and satisfying himself that everything was going as he wished—not that he had expected otherwise with Mark as his straw boss—he went on, "Shall we go inside and set a spell while we talk things out?"

"I always believed it's folly to stand when one can sit and absolute madness to sit when one can—!" April began, then gave a merry smile and continued quickly, "I'd better not finish *that*."

"You're worried about Wils and Stone going to Prescott," Margaret guessed after she had taken the blonde and the small Texan into the

95

sitting room—which she already knew well enough to be able to negotiate without needing assistance from Steffie or Rollo—and indicated the chairs for them to use. "Aren't you?"

"That's part of it," Dusty admitted. "There're a few things about what happened yesterday that don't sit right with me."

"Such as?" April prompted.

"I could go for just the one bunch coming to do something they were hired for without meeting the feller who did it, then not having found out he was already dead before they set in to doing it," the small Texan said. "But two lots making the same mistake doesn't sit right with me any more than those *hombres* who, from what Calam said they were figuring on doing, sound like real mean sons of—not real *nice* to know—showing up to start running the cantina as a going concern again the way they have. There's been nothing said around town to show anybody knew *that* was coming off, nor enough trade going around for them to even figure one would pay them."

"They could have made sure it was kept a secret," April pointed out. She had noticed that the dusty-blond Texan still retained his disinclination to employ profanity in the presence of women.

"In fact, I'd say they'd do all they could to keep it that way. From what I learned about the saloon game before Wils saved me from a life of sin, I don't reckon they'd want a well-established business rival, particularly one who had been around town long enough to have got on good terms with the local law, to know they were figuring to come and cut in on his business."

"I yield to your superior knowledge, ma'am," Dusty claimed, partially rising to give a quick bow and receiving what would have been a curtsy if the blonde had moved sufficiently far from her seat to complete it. "Only, I don't like coincidences, and there've been too many of them just recently."

"So you think the trouble we've been having might not be over after all?" Margaret suggested. "But the man who was behind it is dead."

"Eisteddfod got made wolf bait, along with his boss gun," Dusty replied. "Only, I'm starting to wonder whether he was the big chief in the game, or just one of the little Indians. Should it be the last, we might not be out of the dark and piny woods yet."

"And you think there might be danger to Stone and Wils on the way to Prescott?" April asked.

"Let's put it this way," the small Texan answered quietly. "I'd sooner be safe than sorry. So, if you give me the go to it, I'm going to send Lon and Kiowa to follow them without being seen."

"Why not just send somebody lickety-split to tell them what you think?" the blonde wanted to know.

"Because they have to get to the Land Agent at the capital and make their bids before word gets out about there being two prime spreads likely up for grabs down here," Dusty replied. "And, knowing them, they wouldn't go if they thought there could be danger to you."

"And you think there may be?" Margaret queried, her face pointed straight at the small Texan as if she were able to see him.

"Like I said," Dusty drawled, "I'd a whole heap rather be safe than sorry. And I reckon we can keep you both safe without needing two nervous mother-hen husbands underfoot. Thing being about that, April, I'd sooner have you stay on here." Seeing the way in which the blonde stiffened, he held forward his right hand in a placating gesture and went on, "Now, don't get all riled and ready for dish-throwing. I know you can count on Jimmy Conlin and the rest of your boys. Only, there's none of them has had the experience that Waggles, Chow, Silent, and Peaceful have gathered over the years. Comes trouble, they'd be ready to do everything up to getting killed to keep you safe, but there's not one of them has needed to pick up the fight-savvy those four have gathered riding trail herds with the Wedge."

"I hate to have to say this, April," Margaret put in, "but I think Dusty is right."

"You should wash your mouth out with lye soap for saying such a thing," the blonde declared. "And I know he's acting for the best as he sees it, but I don't want Jimmy and the boys to figure I didn't trust them when things might go hard."

"There isn't any reason why they should ever know," Margaret replied. "You could send for your maid and allow you're going to lend a hand looking after me while Steffie goes on being midwife for Child City."

"You *don't* send me there for safety," the ash-blonde stated, having been listening to all that was said. "The day I'm too scared to stand by my friends root, hawg, or die is the day I'll run home to Momma. And don't say Tildy Canoga needs watching over. When I deliver 'em, they stay delivered and don't need my gentle touch to keep them going. Anyways, April needs me here to help her get things going for our show in town."

"And you can have us mother-henned here better than needing to make work for Amon Reeves by having to keep an eye on Steffie in town, Dusty," the older blonde pointed out. "He's likely to have enough work without needing that added to it."

Seeing that the other two women were showing concurrence with what April said, the small Texan concluded that he had about as much chance of changing their respective and collective minds as he would have if he was in contention against his cousin Betty back home to the OD Connected.

"Like I said before, ladies, calf rope," Dusty drawled. "Only, do I have your go to it for sending Lon and Kiowa after your husbands?"

"You may as well," April said, contriving to sound as though she was granting a favor.

"I agree," Margaret supported. "We've so many shiftless loafers around here that two less won't be noticed."

What none of the group knew was that, at that moment, a rider from Child City was coming to tell how Sheriff Amon Reeves had been shot and seriously wounded in the early hours of the morning and to deliver a request from Counselor Edward Sutherland to speak with Dusty on a matter of the greatest importance.

I WANT THE HIDE OF
WHOEVER DID IT

"I'm sorry to have to bring you into town like this, Captain Fog," Counselor Edward Sutherland apologized. "But I didn't know where else to turn. You made good time getting here."

"We rode relay all the way," the small Texan replied, but he could not help feeling uneasy over the fact that he had left the care of hard-pushed horses to somebody else, though he knew the persons who had volunteered for the task to be competent and the reason justifiable.

"You'll need the Kid to help you look for sign," the attorney said, nodding his head in approval. He had been told that Dusty and two other riders were coming, and when he heard more than one set of footsteps approach the sheriff's office, he had concluded that the Kid had accompanied Fog.

"He isn't with me," Dusty stated flatly, and thought he detected a suggestion of annoyance mingled with disappointment on Sutherland's far-from-expressive florid face. He found this puzzling.

The arrival of the news about Sheriff Amon Reeves having been shot did not reach the Wedge ranch until after the Ysabel Kid and Kiowa Cotton had set off on the mission to which they had been assigned. Upon hearing what had happened, the small Texan had guessed why Sutherland had asked him to go to Child City with all speed. However, he had decided that he must not call either of the part-Indian members of Ole Devil Hardin's floating outfit from the task they were given. His every instinct, in which he had complete faith, had warned that what had happened to the peace officer was tied in with the incidents of the previous day. Therefore, he had concluded that there was now an even greater need for Stone Hart and Major Wilson Eardle to have the support of two such competent fighting men should the need arise. Also, he had settled in his own mind how he must deal with the present situation.

Faced with such a situation, some men might have told Margaret Hart and April Eardle what was suspected and asked for their opinion on how best to deal with it. That was not the way Dusty Fog had been raised, nor had he even given a thought to doing so. Instead, he had reached his own conclusions and set about acting on them without calling upon anybody else to give him support. He did not doubt for a moment that Mark Counter was fully capable of replacing him as roundup captain. However, there was the matter of who was to take over as straw boss. The way he produced the solution was a tribute to his intelligence and knowledge of human nature.

After telling the women what he intended to do, the small Texan had called upon them to assist him. Every one of the foremen connected with the roundup was sufficiently experienced to take over as straw boss, but he wanted to avoid any appearance that one was being favored over the others. He had known how such an accusation could be avoided and immediately put his ideas into effect. Fortunately, the men he wanted from the AW, Arrow P, and the Vertical Triple E ranches were still close enough that he could recall them, so he had sent a message with Tarbrush.

The reps appointed by each spread had returned, and Dusty had had them brought into the sitting room of the Wedge's main house. Explaining his reason for not going straight out to the place appointed for the roundup to start and why the need he was likely to be absent from his duties could arise, the response to the news was indicative of the high regard in which the sheriff was held by the local men. Then he had had April go from the room and return with three long and one short straws. She had Steffie Willis hold them and Margaret—whom the pair from the Arrow P and Vertical Triple E ranches knew to be blind and therefore unable to show bias even if such was the intention—performed the selection.

Although nothing in his attitude had shown how he felt, the small Texan was pleased that the short straw was drawn by Jimmy Conlin of the AW, giving him the right to be straw boss. He did not doubt that, like the rest of the crew, Steven Baird was what in cow-country terms was called a saint—an honest hand—despite having been employed by Eustace Edgar Eisteddfod. However, he wanted to allow both foremen to stay in charge of their respective spreads until—as yet it was not known whether either previous owner had made arrangements for his property to be passed via a will—the matter of continued ownership was settled. April had stated that she had no objections to reducing the strength of the guard force at her home, since she believed that those who remained could handle any situation that arose. Furthermore, the reps for the spread whose owners had died had declared they were satisfied with the result and left to rejoin the roundup.

When asked by April whom he was to take with him to Child City, since he would require competent assistance should he have called the play right with regard to the reason Sutherland had sent for him, Dusty had paused before replying. Much to his gratification, as he had known whom he would choose under different circumstances, he had the matter resolved for him in no uncertain fashion.

"Take Rusty, like you want to," Steffie had said, drawing the correct conclusion as to why the small Texan had glanced her way instead of replying immediately. "If you reckon I expect him to be kept wrapped up in cotton just 'cause I was good enough to marry him, you can think again, Cap'n Fog. He's worn a badge under you afore, more fool him, so he could be the backing you need. Only, should you both get killed while you're doing it, I'll *never* speak to either of you again."

Amused by the ash-blonde's last comment, which was typical cowhand humor, Dusty had accepted the offer with gratitude. As Steffie had said, her husband had served as a deputy town marshal under him and had proved to be competent. His second choice of assistant drew looks of surprise from the three men, but was to be the source of great satisfaction to Thorny Bush. He had made the selection because he had been impressed by the way in which the youngster dealt with the situation in the Arizona State

Saloon. When Margaret had questioned Thorny's youth, Dusty had said that—in addition to believing that Bush would be reliable support—he felt the experience gained could prove of use in later years.

With the matter settled, Rusty had arrived accompanied by Bush, who did all he could to prevent his elation and pride from showing, and no time had been wasted before Dusty and the other two set out for Child City. To enable them to move at a good speed for a long distance, each of them rode a two-horse relay chosen from the Wedge's *remuda;* the horses were less use than others where working cattle was concerned, so they would not be missed. In addition to the animals he selected, the small Texan took along his big paint stallion; he knew the need for its proven reliability under all kinds of conditions might arise.

The journey was completed with alacrity, made possible because all three Texans were skilled at riding and were well-mounted. On arrival, wanting to see to the needs of the hard-pressed animals regardless of how pressing the situation might be, the need for them to do so personally did not arise. Indicative of the continued less-than-amicable state of affairs between Calamity Jane and the men who claimed ownership of the old *cantina,* Dobe Killem's wagons were parked outside the livery barn and their teams stood in the larger of its corrals. Knowing her well and appreciating her many good qualities, Dusty had at first regarded her presence with mixed feelings. However, as had happened on other occasions, he soon felt gratitude for her having had to stay on in Child

City until the balance of payment owed to her boss was received. The reason given for the delay was that the money must be obtained from the Cattlemen's Bank, and it was closed for the day by the time the work of unloading was completed.

Saying she could guess why the small Texan had come, having spent the previous evening involved in the lively times that ensued at the saloon—in fact, having sparked some of them off, although for once avoiding conflict with any of the female employees—the redhead had offered to help in every way she could. The first task, which she suggested immediately, was to care for the horses and save Dusty any further delay in going to see Sutherland. On being given permission to do this, she assigned the work to her fellow drivers, all of whom hovered in the background and showed a willingness to do as they were told.

Calamity had delegated the labor so that she might accompany the small Texan should she be needed. Showing that she had specific suspects in mind, she had said that the women who were to work at the *cantina* were not much of an improvement over the bosses and male employees. This, she had declared, was one of the reasons it had apparently been decided by Derek Hatton and Steven's own wagon in which the distaff side of their party had traveled had followed about four hours behind those hired from Killem. Sensing that the presence of the redhead could prove useful, Dusty had agreed to her proposal.

With the welfare of the horses in hands he knew to be capable, Dusty proceeded on foot to the appointed rendezvous. Not unexpectedly, there had been considerable interest shown in his party during the walk from the livery barn to the jailhouse. Nor, he suspected, was it entirely due to seeing the redhead clad in her usual fashion when accompanying him.

Rather, it arose from the citizens either knowing or guessing why he had been asked to come. Leaving the others on the porch and going into the sturdily constructed building, he had found it to differ only in minor essentials from all the others he had seen during his travels around the range country, and because of its well-cared-for state, it could have been the one from which his father operated as the sheriff of Rio Hondo County. He found that, in addition to Sutherland, big, bulky, white-haired, and Germanic-looking Doctor Klaus Gottlinger and a leathery-faced old-timer in worn yet clean range clothes with a badge of office pinned to his calfskin vest were present.

"Is that other man of your floating outfit along, then?" the attorney asked. "I've heard the Wedge crew speak of him as a damned good scout, but we've never met, and, I'm sorry to admit, I can't bring his name to mind."

"It's Kiowa Cotton," Dusty supplied, knowing that no deliberate slight to the Indian-dark and dangerous-looking member of the OD Connected ranch was intended. "I had to send him along with Lon. Anyways, if there should be the need for reading sign, I've heard Burt Alvord is passing fair along those lines."

"He's also not in town," Sutherland growled.

"Reckoned Amon'd said for him to go to Fort

Mescalero on some errand when he come in here and collected all his gear," said the elderly man, Liam Fox, who served as jailer for the sheriff. "I've never seed him so all-fired eager to do nothing 'cepting draw his pay afore."

"Would that be soon after word got around about what had happened to the sheriff?" Dusty inquired, knowing the man in question had worked for a time in the employment of his uncle, Texas John Slaughter, and left with a flimsy excuse on an occasion when danger threatened.

"You're right as the Injun side of a hoss, Cap'n Fog," Fox confirmed. "And I don't somehow reckon as he'll be coming back."

"And if he does, he'll soon be leaving again!" the attorney stated grimly. "Good riddance to bad rubbish is how I see it."

"How come Amon hired him?" Dusty inquired.

"Needed a feller could read sign and is a whole heap more spry'n me," the jailer supplied before either of the other local men could speak. "And the pay here don't come so high that Amon could be overchoosy."

"There wasn't much need for high-priced help to enforce the law around the town or County," the attorney said in the dry Scottish burr that had become second nature to him when discussing money matters. "In fact, there were *some*, present company excepted, Doc, who reckoned having a deputy as well as a jailer was a needless expense."

"Likely," the small Texan said in a noncommittal tone, then got down to business. "And

I'm ready to take over for Amon until he's back on his feet, gentlemen. Because that's why you've sent for me, unless I miss my guess."

"It is, Captain Fog, it is," Sutherland confirmed. "Amon's a good friend as well as a damned fine peace officer, and I want the hide of whoever did it."

"And I'll do my damnedest to see you get it," Dusty promised. "Only, I'm going to need some help. No offense to you, Seth, but I've got me that said help waiting outside."

"And, speaking in my capacity as Justice of the Peace for Spanish Grant County, they're hired as your deputies," the attorney stated without hesitation. "Now, what can we do for you?"

"Tell us what happened," Dusty requested after he had called his companions in and introduced them to the local men.

"All we know is Amon was found by a feller on his way home from Widow Bosworth's house," Sutherland obliged. "Give him his due, though he's a married man, he didn't let where he'd been stop him coming to let me know. There wasn't enough light for us to make a search for clues right then. All we could do was have Doc Gottlinger here come and 'tend to Amon, then move him to his place."

"Any notion what kind of gun was used, sir?" Bush asked before any more could be said. He had read of a similar question asked in one of the many blood-and-thunder books he secretly enjoyed.

"I might be less use than decoration at a child-birth, as I hear I was described by *somebody* recently," Gottlinger growled, eyeing the youngster in a less-than-amiable fashion. His accent was that of a New Englander and had only a hint of his Germanic origins. Glancing at Rusty more in amusement than anger, he went on, "Whoever might be fool enough to marry that said *somebody* would have all my sympathy. Anyway, as I wasn't at a childbirth and decided it might be a good idea, I got the bullet out without too much difficulty. I'll admit that I had a mite of luck there. Amon's muscled like an ox and he was only hit by something around a .38 caliber, certainly not anything as heavy as a .44-.40, nor even .44-.28. It took him just under his right shoulder blade from behind, and I found it just under the skin of his chest. It's a bad wound and will keep him off his feet for a spell, but I'm pretty near certain he will live."

"You've no idea where it was fired from, Doc?" Dusty inquired. He knew the two .44 calibers mentioned to be very common; they were the cartridges for which the Winchester Model of 1873 and its predecessor, the Model of 1866, were chambered.

"No," Gottlinger admitted. "He'd been hit in the back, as I said, and was lying facedown. Which presupposes whoever did it was not in the woods around the Widow's house, although that does not narrow the field down much."

"We'll take a look out where he was found," the small Texan stated. "Not meaning any offense to you, Doc."

"None taken," Gottlinger assured. "That's *your* line of work. Mine is being less use than decoration around a childbirth."

"Should I ever find out who said it and was a braver man, sir," Rusty drawled, "I'd surely take her—whoever it was—to task for saying such a thing."

"I thank you for the sentiment," Gottlinger claimed with a frosty smile. "And I know exactly how you feel. I too made the foolish mistake of marrying a trained nurse."

"Did Amon follow the same rounds every time he made them?" Dusty asked, bringing the conversation back to a serious level despite having found the brief exchange amusing, as did the others present.

"Well, not foot for foot and as regular as clockwork," Sutherland replied, without going on to say that the sheriff was too experienced a peace officer to make such a basic mistake. "But I reckon anybody who'd been around for a while could guess roughly where he'd be about when."

"Those two sons of bitches down to the *cantina* wouldn't've been around long enough to find out," Calamity said in a bitter tone. "Only, I'll bet they've been in enough fuss one place and another to be able to make a real good guess at where they'd find the local law making his rounds. It's not as if this is such a big place there'd be a whole slew of choices."

"Why do you think they might have been involved, Calam?" the attorney inquired. He had learned the previous evening that the girl preferred to be addressed in such a fashion rather than as "miss."

"Less I miss my guess about 'em," the redhead replied, "they wouldn't be too all-fired keen to have a smart and honest gent like I've heard the sheriff to be running the law when they start their place going. Was I asked, I'd put my money on them being along."

"And we'll go talk to them after we've looked around where the shooting happened," Dusty stated. "Damn it, I wish now I hadn't sent both Lon and Kiowa off."

"Tumac's a pretty fair hand at reading sign as well as driving a team," Calamity declared. "You can call on him for anything needs doing."

"*Bueno*," the small Texan answered, and was grateful for the offer. "Now, if you'll get us sworn in, Counselor, we'll make a start."

"*All* of you?" Sutherland asked, glancing at the expectant redhead.

"*All* of us," Dusty confirmed. "Could be there's going to be the need to deal with womenfolks along the trail, and I'd sooner have one, which they do reckon Calam is, than let my men do it." With the swearing-in ceremony completed and badges of office pinned in place, he went on, "All right, *deputies,* let's go get her done."

"Straight to the *cantina*?" Calamity inquired hopefully.

"*After* we've taken a look around where the shooting happened, like I said," Dusty answered. "There's nothing to prove they were mixed up in the shooting, no matter how mean and crooked *you* might reckon them to be. There could be others around town who don't take kind to the sheriff, leave us not forget."

"If there are, I can't bring any of them to mind," Sutherland stated, and the other two local men nodded their concurrence. "Hell, he was even liked by the fellers from the ranches and Fort Mescalero he had to toss in jail for being drunk or over-rowdy. They used to reckon the breakfast Libby Reeves served up was better than they got wherever it was they'd come from."

"Which only leaves those bastards at the *cantina*," the redhead stated in the manner of one who felt herself vindicated in an assumption.

"They're a *possibility,* no more and no less," Dusty pointed out. "And that's how they'll be treated when we call on them."

"Do we do said calling like in Quiet Town, Dusty?" Rusty inquired, and now there was no suggestion of levity in his voice.

"*Just* like Quiet Town, *amigo,*" the small Texan confirmed, guessing what was implied by the question. "Which you, taking on as first deputy, know what's wanted."

"Get a scatter from the rack and some buckshot shells, Thorny, and the same for me," Rusty ordered, and seeing the youngster make a gesture toward the butts of the two ivory-handled Colts on his gunbelt, continued, "If those two *hombres* and their hired help're as mean 'n' ornery as Calam reckons, which I don't figure she's making a wild guess, you'll find a scatter licks the hell out of a handgun for making them act all peaceable."

"I'll go along with you," the redhead declared, then gestured with the Winchester Model of 1873 carbine in her right hand. "Only, me being just a weak 'n' defenseless li'l gal, I'll rely on this here saddelegun and my ole bullwhip should trouble come. If that's all right with you, First Deputy?"

"I allus go along with whatever any weak 'n' defenseless li'l gal like you wants," Rusty as-

112

serted. "Take whatever you figure you need best."

"By cracky!" Calamity declared. "I see that Steffie's raising you right 'n' proper now she's got you hooked 'n' landed. There's a gal I can right easy get to like."

In the light of certain future events, the redhead would find she had no reason to reverse the opinion.

YOU TRY TO STOP HIM

"Well, this is where it happened, but there's nothing close by to say who did it," Dusty Fog remarked as he stood with his recently appointed female and two male deputies near the place where Sheriff Amon Reeves had been found lying seriously wounded. "Do you reckon Tumac would do some looking around and see if he can find any sign to help, Calam?"

Counselor Edward Sutherland had had the outline of the injured man marked with what appeared to be the blue chalk used on pool cues before he was moved, a precaution showing considerable foresight, as such a technique was not yet much practiced, especially by Western peace officers. This had allowed the position where he fell to be easily located. However, there was nothing in the immediate vicinity to suggest the point at which the shot was fired. Accepting his own limitations where carrying out such a task was concerned and lacking the skill that either the Ysabel Kid or Kiowa Cotton could have provided, the small Texan had no hesitation before requesting that the search for a sign be performed by somebody better qualified than himself. Moreover, aware of their own shortcomings in that direction, he knew his three companions would have no objections to his proposal.

"If he says he won't," Calamity Jane replied, "I'll talk to him all sweet, polite, 'n' reasonable, while I'm telling him to get to doing it afore I whomp his li'l ole pumpkin head with a shovel."

"*That's* sweet, polite, 'n' reasonable?" Thorny Bush inquired, looking the redhead over with frank and open admiration as he wondered, not for the first time, if there could possibly be another woman like her.

"You should meet Dusty's cousin Betty," Rusty Willis stated. He had done so at one of General Ole Devil Hardin's famous Christmas Turkey Shoots and concluded that the members of the OD Connected ranch crew had not exaggerated when they described the way she had ruled their lives by wielding a hand they cheerfully affirmed made steel feel softer than melting butter.

"Why, they do say she can come close to being unsweet, less'n polite, and nowheres near close to reasonable when she's so minded. Fact being, I did hear tell as how she got grabbed by a bunch of owlhoots to be held for ransom 'n' they was so plumb discouraged by the way she treated 'em, they sent her back with one."

"Don't you believe him, Thorny," Calamity advised. "Steffie hasn't got him out of spinning windies *yet*. Anyways, Betty's just as sweet 'n' kindhearted as I am."

"Which being," the youngster stated vehemently, tensing and ready to take whatever steps necessary to avoid the consequences over what he meant to say next, "I surely hope as how I never run across her."

"If you three don't stop wasting the good taxpaying citizens of Spanish Grant County's happily-parted-with money," Dusty growled with mock severity, knowing the remarks were a way his companions were working off their frustrations over being unable to find anything helpful, "you're right soon going to wish you'd never run across *me*. Let's get over to make talk with those jaspers at the cantina."

"We'll have to do it, fellers," the redhead informed the male deputies, and went on as if letting them in on a strictly kept secret, "He outranks us, you know."

They took the shortest route to their destination—with Bush informing the others that if being a peace officer called for so much walking he was going back to working cattle—and were almost within sight of the building when they heard the sound of dogs fighting. Advancing quickly, they saw a large black animal with ragged ears and only a short stump of a tail savaging one smaller and of equally indeterminate breed. Making the most of its heavier weight and bulk, it was on top with its jaws clamped upon the throat of its victim. Close by, the youngster who had brought the news of the birth at the Sutherland house and Calamity's arrival was holding his right forearm, which was bleeding from a bite, while yelling at the two owners of the cantina to make the attack stop.

"If that's your dawg, *hombre*," Dusty snapped, advancing faster than any of his companions, "call it off!"

"Ole Buster wouldn't take no telling from me, nor Der'," Steven Scott answered, directing only a casual glance at the small Texan. "*You* try to stop him if you want it doing."

Without bothering to reply, and inadvertently getting in Calamity's way as she transferred the Winchester Model of 1873 carbine to her left hand with the intention of using the right to draw and use her whip, Dusty darted forward. He grabbed the black dog by the back of the neck and base of the attenuated tail. Feeling the powerful muscles under the skin of the throat, he knew he would avail himself nothing by applying pressure in an attempt to make the jaws release their victim, so he delivered a kick to the kidney region. He could not bring himself to use his full power knowing that to do so might cause serious injury, or even death. Nevertheless, the impact was sufficient to elicit a snarling yelp that caused the other dog's throat to be released. Then, with a surging heave that was testimony to his Herculean muscular development, he swung around just as swiftly and flung the beast away from him.

"What the he—!" Derek Hatton snarled, watching what was happening and starting to reach for his revolver.

"Leave it *there*!" Rusty commanded, swinging the shotgun he had borrowed from the sheriff's office into alignment and drawing back both hammers.

"And *you*!" Bush supplemented, duplicating Rusty's movement.

"The rest of you sons of bitches stay put!" Calamity bellowed at the full power of her lungs, forgetting the whip and bringing the carbine to shoulder level while working the lever in a blur of motion and directing the barrel toward the employees of the duo who showed signs of coming to their employers' assistance. "Else some of you'll be picking point forty-four-caliber lead out'n your navels!"

Every one of the group came to an immediate halt. Having traveled in her company for some time, they did not doubt that the attractive and shapely redhead meant what she said and possessed the skill needed to make good the threat. What was more, proving the selection of how the visit to the cantina should be made had been correct, neither of the owners being covered by the male deputies—who they assumed to be no more than just a chance passing pair of cowhands from Texas, since they had not noticed the badges worn by any of the newcomers—attempted to complete the drawing of the weapons as they had contemplated and commenced. Such was the menace of the shotguns, the dimensions of the twin ten-gauge muzzles seeming even greater than the actual .775 caliber, that the New Englander never noticed that the weapon being pointed at him by the youngster did not have the hammers cocked. Instead, like his companion, he stared as if unable to believe his eyes at what was happening a short distance away.

Landing on its feet, Buster let out a roaring snarl. As would all too often prove the case with the American pit-bull terriers that developed from such out-crosses as produced it, the black dog did not restrict its savagery to others of its species. Sensing from where the attack upon it had originated, it charged with what in a human being would have been seen as a determination to take revenge. Coming into range, it launched itself from the ground with the intention of closing its jaws on some portion of the small figure's anatomy. It moved with the speed and deadly purpose with which it launched all its attacks, but this time it was up against a vastly more dangerous quarry than any it had ever seen.

Instead of reaching for either or both of his matched bone-handled Colt Civilian Model Peacemakers, which he could have done with equal facility—he had developed a natural tendency to be completely ambidextrous as a boy in Rio Hondo County, Texas, possibly as a subconscious means of distracting attention from his lack of height in a land of generally tall men—Dusty shot out his hands. Using the same kind of precision he employed to make him so deadly a shot with his revolvers, he caught the dog just above the feet of the forelegs and wrenched them apart with a force equal to that exerted when flinging it aside. The dog's hideous roar of rage turned into a scream of agony as he did so. Then, with another surging swung, he flung Buster from him once more. Upon landing, its heart having been ruptured by the force the pulling apart of the legs had exerted upon its torso, it started to writhe in torment.

Aware of what he was almost certain to do when coping with the attack by the dog in such a fashion, a sense of rage filled the small Texan. He had never taken any pleasure in inflicting pain on dumb animals. Nor did knowing that he was in contention against a creature conditioned to attack, even kill, without compunction make his anger any less. He was aware that the dog's inborn trait of viciousness had been deliberately developed by the man who owned it, and that was where he intended to vent his feelings. For once in his life, he was in the kind of a mood that made the Ysabel Kid so deadly and efficient a warrior in the way of the Pehnane Comanche Dog Soldier.

"Whose dawg is it?" Dusty demanded, turning toward the owners of the cantina.

"*His!*" Hatton yelped, showing all the instincts of a rat deserting a sinking ship. He was getting the word out before his companion could direct responsibility his way.

"Come over here and put it out of its suffering!" the small Texan commanded, but he no longer struck either of the men as being short in stature. "Do it *pronto,* damn you, or you'll find what *suffering* gets caused when you're gut-shot!"

Staring in horror at Dusty, as other men had done, Scott felt he was not up against a living human being. What stood before him was a large killing machine primed and waiting to fulfill the sole purpose behind its construction. It was a trait Bush had never suspected of the small Texan, a man he revered more than any other except one. Nor had either Calamity—who was leaving her companions to keep control over the saloon workers, now that they no longer needed to watch Hatton or Scott, so she could go and give attention to the injured boy—nor Rusty seen Dusty in such a frame of mind. In fact, even the small Texan was unaware of how great a change his mood had wrought in his demeanor. All he knew was that he intended to have his demand met, or the man to whom it was made would pay the consequences.

"You go lend him a hand should it be needed," Dusty ordered Hatton as—letting out something close to a sob—Scott stumbled toward the spot where the dog still writhed in agony on the ground.

Trying to speak and finding that words would not come, the man dressed as a gambler went after his partner on less than steady legs. Both of them drew their revolvers and, controlling their hands only with difficulty, sent bullets into the stricken dog, bringing its suffering to an end. Then they swung around and saw Dusty approaching with a bearing charged with menace. Even though the Texan came with empty hands, neither man could retain hold of his revolver, much less try to lift it into alignment. Instead, they stood staring very much like a cottontail rabbit mesmerized by a coiled and ready-to-strike rattlesnake. Each found himself unable to move or speak under the gaze of those coldly watching gray eyes.

Suddenly the small Texan shot forward his clenched right hand. However, the way he had it folded was different from the method usually employed. Sent with the same precision Dusty had shown when catching hold of the dog by the forelegs, the protruding knuckle of the first finger made contact just beneath the center of Scott's unlovely nose. Grinding into the collection of nerve centers known as the philtrum that lay so vulnerable beneath the thin covering of skin, the blow caused such a wave of agony to rip through the gambler-clad man that he could not give so much as a cry of suffering before he collapsed to roll near the body of the dog, both hands clasped to his face.

Giving Hatton no time to recover from the shock caused by seeing what had happened to Scott, Dusty turned attention and aggressive action his way. Again, the small Texan did not employ a conventional means of attack. Instead of folding his left hand into a fist, he kept it open with fingers together and thumb bent across its palm. Coming around with a chopping motion, the edge of the hand slammed into the front of Hatton's throat like an ax being driven against a piece of wood. To the recipient of the latest attack in the fashion Dusty had been taught by Ole Devil Hardin's valet—a small Oriental whom most people thought to be Chinese, but actually hailed from the still little-known islands of the Japanese Empire—it seemed that he had indeed been hit by an ax. Gagging and scarcely able to breathe, he stumbled in a half-circle, then sank to his knees with fingers chafing ineffectually at his windpipe as he sought to ease his suffering.

"All right, you bunch!" Dusty said, kicking aside the two weapons discarded by his victims in a way that rendered them unusable until they had received a thorough cleaning. "I want to see all the guns you've got, and I mean *every* one!"

"Where is the sheriff?" inquired the medium-size, scrawny, although well-dressed man who had come into the office of the jailhouse, looking in a disdainful fashion to where Dusty Fog was seated behind the desk.

After dealing with the men hired to work at the old *cantina* without finding what he was hoping he would, Dusty and his deputies, with able and willing support from the presence of Counselor Edward Sutherland in the capacity of the Justice of the Peace for Spanish Grant County, carried out an inspection of every other weapon in Child City without finding one capable of delivering the wound received by Amon Reeves. On being questioned, the owner of Clitheroe's General Emporium had stated that he had neither sold a weapon nor had ever stocked ammunition in a caliber of the kind that Doctor Klaus Gottlinger claimed had been used to wound Sheriff Amon Reeves.

Leaving Rusty Willis and Thorny Bush to check through supplier catalogues produced by Amos Clitheroe, the small Texan, Calamity Jane, and the lawyer had returned to the jailhouse to await the results of the search by the male deputies. Sutherland had just gone to the backhouse when the visitor entered.

"That's me," Dusty answered in a tone that suggested he was embarrassed rather the gratified at making the admission.

"But I was told that *Dusty Fog* had been given the office temporarily," the man stated, running his gaze over the small Texan.

"I have!" Dusty drawled.

"*You* have?" the man repeated. "Are *you* Dusty Fog?"

"If he's not, *mister*," Calamity put in, far from

enamored of the visitor's attitude, "then Dusty's going to be *awful* riled at him, 'cause he slept with Mrs. Dusty Fog on the night of their wedding."

"Oh!" the man snorted, and swung his cold, baleful scowl to the redhead. "And I suppose *you* are Mrs. Dusty Fog?"

"I was once, just for a short spell," Calamity replied, restraining an impulse to let the visitor find out how one of her feet would feel as a teeth brace. "Only, it all ended afore we could get bedded down together good 'n' proper."

"Then *you* are the Dusty Fog who was appointed sheriff?" the man said, still sounding doubtful as he tried to reconcile the man he was addressing with the description he had received of the temporary and well-known sheriff.

"So I was told when I had the badge pinned on," the small Texan replied, taking an immediate dislike to the visitor. "Is there something I can do for you?"

"My name is Nigel Jones," the man introduced himself, in the manner of one declaring himself to be, if not God, at least very high in heaven's hierarchy. Producing a document from his inside left breast pocket, he opened it and laid it on the desk. "As you will see from this, I am a lawyer accepted by the Territorial bar."

"I wonder what kind of liquor he buys there," Calamity Jane said, pitching her voice just loudly enough to make it appear that she had no wish for the visitor to hear her.

"That's what it says, Counselor," Dusty admitted, having giving the document a cursory glance and returned it with a gesture of disinterest. "Like I just said, is there something I can do for you?"

"It is my intention to hang up my shingle in Child City," Jones stated.

"Every town can never have too many law-wranglers around, I always say," the small Texan drawled without so much as a glance at Sutherland, who had returned from the backhouse without being noticed by the other lawyer and was looking at the wanted posters on the notice board at the rear of the office, as if they were of such absorbing interest he was indifferent to everything else.

"I trust you will continue to say so when you hear what brings me *here*!" the newly arrived lawyer stated in a distinctly menacing fashion.

"Then tell up, sir," Dusty offered.

"I have had placed before me a serious allegation that you employed unnecessary and dangerous force against two citizens of this community," Jones declared, then paused.

"Excuse me," the small Texan said, making no attempt to ask the questions that were obviously expected. "But would you be kin to that Eustace Edgar Eisteddfod who was made wolf bait of a spell back?"

"I've never even heard of anybody with that name," Jones declared, his face becoming an inscrutable mask. "Why?"

"He allowed to be Welsh," Dusty elaborated. "And I've heard tell Jones is a right common name there."

"Well, we aren't—*weren't,* as I understand you to imply he is deceased—related, or even acquainted," the lawyer stated. "Nor would it be anything to do with why I have come here even if we were."

"What did bring you here, Counselor?" the small Texan inquired with an assumed innocence even the Kid would have been hard-pressed to better.

"Don't trifle with me, Sheriff, or you'll find it will prove the worst for *you!*" Jones warned, although he was starting to feel very uneasy. He had commenced the interview thinking he was dealing with a naive young deputy hired because of family or some other connection to the Rio Hondo gunfighter who had replaced Reeves. Now he was sure that he was up against the genuine article. Nor, as had happened with many another person before him, did he any longer think of Dusty as being small. "I am here to render a serious complaint against you and your deputies in behalf of my clients."

"If you mean those two *hombres* I had words with down by the cantina," Dusty said, and suddenly his voice took on a note of chilling intensity, "I'd say they got no more than they asked for and deserved. They'd got a damned big dog that they'd let set on a boy's pet and was like' to kill it. Then neither of them would call it off, so I did like they said I should and went to do it. And I did it the only way I could."

"That isn't what *they* tell me," Jones asserted.

"Did you figure it would be?" the small Texan countered.

"Are you saying the way in which you struck them down while they were unarmed and defenseless was justified?"

"Now, that all depends on one's point of view."

"Excuse me, Counselor," Sutherland put in, strolling over to the desk. "Are you acting for the two men who claim to be new owners of the cantina?"

"They *are* the new owners, and have documents to prove it," Jones replied, looking at the local lawyer's attire, which appeared more suitable for a day's hunting than for a member of the legal profession. "Although I don't see how it comes to be any of *your* affair. Who are you?"

"Just another humble member of the bar," Sutherland replied, and continued in an apparently bland fashion, "currently, in my capacity of Justice of the Peace for Spanish Grant County, preparing to handle a charge leveled at them by the man whose son was attacked and had his pet almost killed by their dog."

"Are there any witnesses to say their dog inflicted the bite?" Jones asked.

"I saw the boy's arm when I started to 'tend to it," Calamity stated, eyeing the newcomer in a fashion that implied she would be willing to step into the alley with him to settle the matter tooth and claw if he doubted her word. "Top of that, Doc Gottlinger allowed if it wasn't a dawg bite he'd never seen one when he took over from me. Which, 'cepting the young 'n's pet, there was only the one dawg anywheres close by. So, one way and 'nother, I'd say there's what *some* might call witnesses."

"I think, under the circumstances, Counselor, you may feel that a trial before my court might be prejudicial to your clients," Sutherland remarked in his most legalistic fashion. "Therefore, as is your right, you would prefer that

126

another venue was selected. I am in complete accord with this. It will allow me to take up the side of the gentleman whose boy and dog were injured by that of your client, as I have been requested to do."

"Perhaps the matter can be settled out of court?" Jones hinted with the air of someone who knew all the cards were stacked against him.

"I'm all in favor of doing so," Sutherland asserted in the fashion of a man who was certain he had won. "Provided your clients are willing to make suitable restitution to my client and withdraw their complaints against Sheriff Fog. I feel this is most imperative. As you are probably aware, there are members of our profession who will use any means in their power to defame officers of the law, and I feel it incumbent upon me to ensure nothing of the kind happens to Captain Fog or his deputies."

"I'll make sure they do," Jones promised bitterly, thinking of what else he would say to the pair he had been sent to see. Neither Derek Hatton nor Steven Scott was able to speak distinctly, and they claimed their injuries were received at the hands of Dusty Fog—whom they described as being at least six foot six and huge with it—while his deputies kept them covered so they could not fight back. "I'll go and see them straightaway."

"So we've got a new law-wrangler moved in along with a bunch of new saloon folks," Dusty said quietly after Jones had left the office. "I've said all along I don't like coincidences, and they're starting to get too thick on the ground to my way of thinking. Which being, I'm not sorry I sent Lon and Kiowa to keep a watch over Stone and Wils."

OUR EVER-LOVING WIVES DON'T *TRUST* US

"How's your cooking, Stone?" Major Wilson Eardle inquired as he and the owner of the Wedge ranch rode slowly along the stagecoach trail they were following as offering the shortest route to the Arizona Territorial Capital, Prescott. The sun was starting to sink in the west and he had noticed that they were approaching the area of fairly open woodland fringing the Verde River in which they had decided to make camp for the night. "Because mine's not what it used to be and, in fact, it *never* was."

Having left the Wedge ranch early in the morning, each being an excellent rider with long experience in covering long distances in a good time, the two ranchers had contrived to travel at a reasonable speed without pushing their horses too hard. While on their way, they had taken the opportunity—which had not been granted in Child City because of their respective business and social activities, nor when they were with their wives later—to get to know one another better. It had soon become apparent that they were from similar backgrounds and that, if the War Between the States had not intervened, their paths might have crossed earlier. Both had been raised in service families and were destined to make the cavalry their careers. When the issue of secession could not be resolved by peaceful means, neither had been greatly interested in or concerned by the political aspects involved. Even so, Stone Hart had elected to join many of his Southern contemporaries to fight for the Confederate cause, while Eardle remained loyal to the Union.

As was the case with others of his background, including Dusty Fog—although he had not yet attended the United States Military Academy at West Point, as was intended by his family—Stone had seen his promising career as a soldier ended by the meeting at the Appomattox Courthouse between Generals Ulysses Simpson Grant for the Union and Robert Edward Lee in behalf of the South, bringing a gradual cessation of military conflict. Returning to find his home state impoverished and suffering under the evil yoke of what was called Reconstruction, he had turned his attention to the cattle business, by which solvency was brought back to Texas on "hide and horn." Instead of owning land—his family's property having been taken over by legally backed Yankee carpetbaggers for nonpayment of taxes before he came back—he had specialized in leading trail drives for ranchers who lacked enough longhorn cattle to make delivering herds of their own a viable prospect.

Eardle had had the misfortune of spending all his service during the War as a member of the New Jersey Dragoons, a locally enlisted volunteer regiment employed upon what—despite their efficiency—remained one of the North's least successful battle fronts because their best efforts could not offset a succession of commanders who were political appointees and less than competent. This had meant he had not been able to rise higher than major in the rapidly reduced United States Army when peace came. Therefore, having come into money and received the unexpected bequest of a ranch, the name of which he had changed to AW in honor of his recently taken wife, he had retired to take up a new occupation. His knowledge of the cattle business was limited, so he was most pleased to gain the friendship of a man who had the necessary experience to make a success of ranching and was willing to share it with him.

Shortly after noon, with a satisfactory number of miles behind them, the pair had made a meal from the food that had been put up by their wives for them to carry "greasy sack" on the packhorse, currently being led by Stone. Resuming the journey, they had continued to talk about matters pertaining to the cattle business in general and to exchange reminiscences about their respective military service without rancor on either's part. Since the man they believed should be held responsible was dead, they had not spoken of the troubles that might have prevented a friendly association between them from taking place.

Moving faster than was possible on a stagecoach, except for short distances in an emergency, the ranchers had passed one Wells Fargo relay station in the middle of the afternoon and estimated that they would not arrive at the next shown on the Army map they were using as a guide before sundown. Therefore, they had decided upon where they would halt for the night. The prospect of having to make camp under the stars instead of indoors had not worried them; both had done so on numerous occasions in the past and expected to in the future. Nevertheless, thoughts of cooked food had provoked the question from the boss of the AW ranch.

"I wouldn't want you to think I'm boasting when I say mine has to be worse, because it's not that good," Stone replied. "Which is how come I took to being a trail boss in the first place. Seeing as how I wasn't in the Army to have it done for me anymore, that way I could have Chow Willicka throw up all my grub for me instead of trying to eat what I'd cooked myself."

"I joined West Point for the same reason," Eardle claimed with a wry grin. "Then, when I was set to come out of the Army I concluded I'd have to get married, as I couldn't cook a lick. Trouble being, as she's right proud to *boast*, April's cooking isn't even as good as mine. I didn't believe her when she used to tell me so. I thought she was only trying to stop me tying the knot."

"Margaret cooks real good," Stone praised truthfully. He was still sufficiently new to married life for him to consider such a comment obligatory when talking with a man for whom he was developing a respect and liking.

"That's one real remarkable lady you've got, Stone."

"Don't I know it, Wils. Only, *she* got *me*."

"*I know just* how you feel," the Major declared in what seemed like a manner redolent of heartfelt suffering except for the grin that accompanied it. "April ran away from me until *she* caught *me*." His tone became genuinely serious as he went on, "I've not said this before, *amigo*, and promise I never will again, but I'll never stop being grateful for the way Margaret and you stood by her straightaway back in Child City."

"Why wouldn't we stand by her? She's one hell of a nice *lady*, and according to what Dusty, Mark, and the Kid told us, she proved way back that she'd made a hand," Stone said, pleased by the use of the Spanish word for friend and giving what amounted to the supreme cowhand accolade for the beautiful blonde. Then he grinned, and, deciding that the conversation had been serious for long enough, he continued, "Whooee! I'd've given good money to have seen those three floating outfit yahoos' faces when they charged in all fierce, warlike, and loaded for bear on you and especially *her* that night."

"It was a sight for sure," Eardle claimed with an equally broad smile, thinking of the aggressive way in which Dusty Fog, Mark Counter, and the Ysabel Kid had entered his home in the belief that he was responsible for various unpleasant incidents, which had culminated with an attempt by a group of hard cases to make off with Margaret Hart. "To put it in a coarse way, they looked like they'd been slapped in the face with an old sock filled with overripe bull droppings when they realized who was ordering them to get their hats off under *her* roof. But seriously, Stone, that whole damned business could have wound up being really bad."

"You've said a whole mouthful, *amigo*," the Texan rancher agreed. "And it would have, sure as sin's for sale in Cowtown, if those sons of bitches'd hurt my li'l gal. I don't reckon even Dusty and Mark together could've stopped the Kid cutting loose like the Pehnane Comanche he can come close to being, even had they a mind to."

"That is one real *hard* young man," the Major assessed, thinking of what he had seen and heard about the Indian-dark, almost always black-clad young Texan with the handsome features that in repose appeared to exude an almost baby-faced innocence.

"They don't come any harder when it's called for, up to and including Kiowa Cotton, him General Hardin loaned me as scout when he heard Johnny Raybold wasn't to hand," Stone supported. "But he's a damned good friend to have by your side when the river's running at full flood and the water's riz way up above the willows. Comes to a point, I've never met one of Ole Devil's floating outfit who wasn't."

"Was I a suspicious man, *amigo,* which nobody could accuse me of being," Eardle remarked in a casual-seeming fashion, noticing that his companion was glancing around in a quick and surreptitious fashion, as had already happened several times during the journey, "I'd say you look a mite *jumpy.*"

"I am," the Texan admitted. "I've got the damnedest feeling we're being watched and followed. There's occasionally been a smidgin of dust stirring behind us and to the right ever since we cleared Spanish Grant County. Only, try as I have, I haven't been able to see hide nor hair of whoever, or whatever, is causing it, if anybody is."

"Could it be Apaches?" the Major suggested. "Corporal Zmijewski said they've been pretty quiet of late hereabouts when we were talking at the Arizona State, which I've often been told is a good time to start looking for them to make a change."

"It could be," Stone conceded. "But if it *isn't*—!"

"Yes?" Eardle prompted.

"I know *two* around and about back to home who're so damned close to being Indians all they need is feathers stuck in their hair and scalps on their belts," the Texan obliged. "Only, *they're* back on the range working their tiny butts off for us rich ranch owners on our roundup while we go gallivanting off on business of more importance than doing it with our own lily-white hands. Or, at least, they're *supposed* to be."

"Why would those two be following us?" the Major asked. He had no need to inquire about the identity of the pair to whom his companion was referring.

"I wouldn't know," Stone confessed. "Unless our ever-loving wives don't *trust* us going off alone to the temptations of the big city."

"*That* can't be it," Eardle denied. "They know we're too loyal, too good at heart, too properly respectful of their feelings—and too damned lily-livered scared they'll beat the hell out of us when we get back home if we did let ourselves be led astray by the temptations of the big city."

"I dearly like a man who's master in his home," the Texan drawled sardonically. "I hope someday I'll meet up with one."

"If you do, let me know so I can come take

a look, because he'll be unique," the Major said. "Anyways, neither Margaret nor April would send *those* particular two to keep an eye on us. They'd be more likely to show us any of the said temptations we couldn't find for ourselves." He paused, then continued, "And, by the way, whoever's dogging our trail are traveling faster than us. The last smidgin of dust I saw was closer up and over to the left."

"Not bad for a Yankee fly-slicer," Stone praised with a grin. He had failed to notice that his companion was carrying out a stealthy watch while he was conducting his own observations. "You must've been timing your sneaky-peeky looks while I was busy taking mine."

"Trust a feller who thought he'd look better to all the Southern belles in cadet gray than honest Union blue to know about sneaky-peeky," Eardle asserted in well-simulated disdain, referring to a confidence trick employed against the unsuspecting in some less-than-scrupulous poker games. "Anyways, leave us not forget I was up against those blasted Johnny Reb Texas Light Cavalry in Arkansas. A man had to learn to play things almost as sneaky-peeky as they did, else he was likely to find out that not all your prisoner-of-war camps treated and fed them as badly as was happening down to Andersonville. I've heard tell that some of our enlisted men and even a couple of officers who were taken in didn't want to come back and live off the rations we were being sent."

"I'd say Ole Devil's line of supply was some shorter than those you Yankees had to rely on where food was concerned, if you had a taste for Texas longhorn beef."

135

"There were some of us who would have *preferred* that to the salted-down lumps of timber our Quartermaster Corps used to send for us to try to eat."

"Leave us not get on to Quartermasters, *please,*" Stone begged like all serving soldiers who had suffered at the hands of that Corps. "I'd sooner try to figure out what we can do about whoever's dogging us *afore* they can get around to doing whatever it is they've been set to dogging us to do."

"That was a bit the long way 'round, even for a Texan," Eardle claimed dryly. "But, like I've heard the old and hairy mountain-men used to say, I'll float my stick along of you. What do you reckon we should do about whose doing the dogging—and where do we get to doing it?"

"They've bedded down right where you reckoned they would, Taos," John Birt said quietly, still seeking to ingratiate himself with his companions after the way he had failed to carry out his seemingly simple task in the Arizona State Saloon in Child City.

"I *knew* they would when they didn't stop over at the last way station," Michael Round declared. "So all we have to do is sneak up on 'em and do what we've been told to do. Just mind you make it look like it was Apache work."

The young hired gun chosen as leader by the three conspirators at the Spreckley Hotel in Prescott and who insisted on being referred to as "Taos Lightning" had just returned through the fairly open woodland fringing the Verde River. In spite of his less-than-flattering feeling toward the three men who had hired him, he was willing to admit that they either had excellent sources of information or, more likely, had made a lucky guess at what was going to happen in Spanish Grant County. He had just returned to where he had left the rest of his party while he rode ahead and located the men he had claimed would be coming along the stagecoach trail on the way to Prescott. He had predicted where their victims would spend the night, and the glow of a fire seen through the trees in the direction he had suggested gave confirmation to the prediction. He had said when deciding upon the action to be taken that it was fortunate he was along to make sure that nothing else could go wrong in the latest work he and the men he had recruited were being paid to carry out. None of the men with him, even Birt, had been enamored of the remark.

Explaining what was to be done when they had come into view of their destination, Round had claimed that each task would be so easily accomplished that there was no need for him to be around while it was being carried out and he had remained outside Child City. Especially when taking into account the less-than-satisfactory—even painful in two cases—way things had turned out, this was far from being a point of view that either the pair supposed to expose April Eardle's background or the quartet instructed to stir up trouble between the cowhands found to their liking. However, none of them were willing to take the lead in calling him to task for the disdain he had shown indiscriminately to them all. Almost as soon as he had brought them together, he had demonstrated how fast he was with a gun. Therefore, despite a mutually shared resentment toward his attitude, not one of them had felt inclined to call him down on the issue in behalf of the others.

"You want for us to take their scalps?" Harold Best inquired, almost hopefully.

"From what I've heard, Apaches don't take scalps," Round answered, delighted by the opportunity to show off his superior wisdom to the less-than-efficient group. "They like other things, like a feller's balls to show off around their wickiups."

"Their hosses and the money they'll likely be carrying is good enough for me," Richard Haigh stated, and looked pointedly at the dandyishly dressed younger man. "Which being, it all gets shared out equal."

"That's for *sure*!" David Blunkett asserted. He also wanted to make sure the point was clear before anything further was done, and the quartet gave muttered indications of concurrence.

"Like you say," Round grunted, too wise to try to take exception to what was clearly a warning even though he had drawn and cocked his right-hand Colt. "Only, we've got to get 'em before sharing can be done. Let's go and do just that."

Knowing what they were going to do, the rest of the group armed themselves in a way each considered most suitable for the purpose. The two older men and Jamie Cann drew Winchester rifles from their saddle boots, but the rest followed the lead of Round by taking out revolvers. Leaving the animals tethered to bushes, they fanned out a little and began to move forward, as silent as they could be. On arriving within clear sight of their destination, they discovered that the precautions they had taken seemed unnecessary. In fact, going by appearances, the men they were planning to rob, kill, and mutilate in a way making it look like the work of Apache warriors had done everything possible to make their work simple.

Having made camp in the center of a fair-size clearing near the ford used by travelers to cross the Verde River at that point, the ranchers had made a large fire, the glow of which had suggested to their attackers where they could be located, and it was still high enough to illuminate them in a most satisfactory manner. The three horses, two excellent for riding purposes and the other obviously having been used to carry the bulky pack panniers standing close to the fire, had been off-saddled and were hobbled near the water's edge in a way that would make flight difficult and render retrieving them a simple matter when the shooting stopped. To further simplify things, there were elongated blanket-covered shapes, one surmounted by a Stetson, and the other, a Burnside campaign hat, indicating that each rancher was sleeping completely oblivious of their danger. Nor was there any sign of whatever weapons they were carrying.

Waiting for the rest of his party to spread farther around in accordance with his orders until they formed almost a half-circle in the undergrowth surrounding the clearing, Round let out what he imagined the war whoop of an Apache warrior would sound like. Having done so, he sprang forward and started to shoot at the nearest shape by the fire, so that he could claim later that it was his lead that brought about the successful mission. Similarly motivated, but the division of the loot as the major consideration, the others were almost as quick at leaving their places of concealment to advance with weapons crashing, further shattering the silence of the night.

Given the surprise they felt sure they had achieved, the hard cases were confident that nothing on this occasion could prevent them from achieving what they had been hired to do.

THERE WILL BE *PANIC* ALL THROUGH THE TOWN

Darting forward, the hired guns eagerly used their weapons to send bullets at what they believed to be victims taken completely unawares.

Disillusionment came swiftly.

Suspecting that whoever was following them might decide to strike that night while they were making camp in the clearing on the western side of the Verde River, as being closer to their destination at Prescott, Stone Hart and Major Wilson Eardle had prepared their ambush accordingly. Hobbling the three horses at a spot they hoped would be out of the line of fire and feeling sure that none would go far, since the grazing was good and all were tired from the exertions of the day, they had collected sufficient dry wood to allow them to build a fire of sufficient size for their purposes. Then they had made two vaguely human shapes with twigs and leaves, covered them with a blanket apiece, and added hats to suggest that they were lying asleep.

Then they had selected the positions in which they intended to lie in wait. Each of them had proved capable of remaining awake through the time that elapsed between completion of their arrangements and their attackers approach through the woodland.

Neither rancher had the slightest compunction over retaliating in kind and without giving prior notice of their presence when the attack was launched. Each knew that the men who dashed into view would have behaved in the same fashion if it had been they and not the dummies lying by the fire. They were equally aware that their assailants would show no hesitation in continuing to try to kill them if offered an opportunity. The Major was given an added incentive to respond when he saw his prized Burnside campaign hat being spun away from the blanket, a hole ripped through its crown by the bullet meant for his head.

The gang were caught in a hail of rifle fire that came from the concealment offered by the trees and bushes flanking the clearing.

Chosen because they had tried to humiliate April Eardle in Child City, and because they were the most easily spotted, David Blunkett and Richard Haigh were the first to be hit. Caught in the center of the chest, Blunkett spun around and involuntarily threw aside his rifle. Almost simultaneously, Haigh was struck between the eyes; he managed to advance a couple of steps while firing another shot before crumpling lifeless to the ground.

Nor did any of the other hard cases fare much better.

Harold Best was killed outright. Each

sustaining a nonfatal injury, John Birt and Thomas Terry also went down. Hit in the right side of his chest so the bullet ranged through and emerged from the other side of his chest without having struck any of the vital organs in passing, Jamie Cann was on the point of throwing aside his weapon and yelling his surrender when he saw Michael Round turn and run, showing no indication of being hurt in any way. Snarling in agony-filled fury, Cann brought up the Winchester carbine he had chosen instead of a revolver. Despite his suffering, and determined to take revenge for Round's impending desertion, he contrived to send lead that shattered the spine and wrote *finis* to the career of Taos Lightning. A moment later, struck twice from widely spaced positions different from those of the ranchers, Cann himself went sprawling facedown, dead in the grass of the clearing.

Concentrating upon what they were doing to the exclusion of everything else, neither Stone nor Eardle had noticed two other rifles being used from separate points along the edges of the open ground.

"Hold hard, Wils!" Stone said urgently, seeing that his companion was on the point of moving forward as the last of their intended attackers was going down. None of them still held a weapon, but he remembered something that had almost passed from his mind and presented an unpleasant possibility. "All these bunch came from *ahead*. Whoever's been dogging us 'most all day were still behind and on each flank last I saw sign of 'em, and there wasn't this many, unless my sighting of the dust they were kicking up on occasion was all wrong."

"Looks like we got telled all wrong, Lon," said a voice the boss of the Wedge ranch had no difficulty in identifying—although his companion did not, if the way the Winchester rifle was swung around was any indication. The voice had originated from the right of the open ground in the undergrowth near the edge of the river. "These gents we was sent to be all protectering for don't need no protectering at all."

"That's for sure as sin's for sale in Cowtown, Kiowa," answered a second Texas drawl from a spot closer to where the ranchers were standing. However, its exact location was impossible to ascertain because of the close to ventriloquial quality that was being given to it. This time, Eardle was also able to identify the unseen speaker. "I don't recollect ever seeing anybody as needed protectering *less,* the sneaky way they laid in wait for those stinking sons of bitches 'n' all. Only, I'm not complaining one li'l mite. It's got us away from that cattle-gathering with Dusty's roundup captain 'n' Mark riding straw boss. One or t'other of 'em'd be *bad* enough, but the two of 'em combined's 'nough to make a man turn white-haired with worry over the amount of work they'd count on having done 'n' all at *once.*"

"Come on out, you blasted pair of Indians!" Stone commanded. "And then you can tell us why you didn't sooner."

"Shuckens," answered the still-unseen Kid. He did not consider it worth saying that, having watched the preparations being made for

143

a few seconds, he had gone forward on foot to find out the extent of the danger to the ranchers. What he had seen suggested that he and his companion could keep their presence undetected until the attack was under way, then play their part in helping to break it up as an unsuspected element. "You gents looked to be having so much fun getting set for these yahoos, we didn't want to go spoiling it."

" 'Sides which, we'd've likely've been give' all the *work*," the first speaker went on, also remaining in concealment. "Us being just hired hands 'n' all."

"Then just why the hell are you *here*?" Stone demanded. "And come on out where I can see what bunch of windies you're going to spin."

"And if it's for the reason I *know* it is," Eardle supplemented. Despite all he had seen and heard of the two men in the woodland, he was impressed by the skill they had shown. Not only had they been following all day without letting more than the odd small clouds of dust be seen, they had contrived to move—undetected by either himself and the other rancher, or the gang who made the attack—into their positions, ready to lend a hand. "You can head straight off back and tell our dear ever-loving wives that we're *fairly* big boys now and don't need any wet-nursing."

"Not *us*, thank you 'most to death," denied the Ysabel Kid as he and Kiowa Cotton strolled, each with his rifle across the crook of his left arm, from their positions at the edge of clearing. "When either of those two ladies as had the misfortune to marry up with you-all tells us to do something, we conclude it's best to up and do it regardless and no matter how much we'd sooner not."

"Being near on a good Christian most times, I'd say amen to that," the other member of General Ole Devil Hardin's floating outfit declared. Matching the Kid in height and much the same build, he too was black-haired. However, his Indian-dark aquiline features were indicative of mixed blood, for all his clothing being that of a cowhand from Texas. "Looks like some of 'em're alive and'll likely be willing to do some telling us things, was they asked *polite 'n' gentle.*"

"How come you've been dogging us all day?" Stone inquired.

" 'Cause we got told to," the Kid answered, as if no further explanation was needed.

"Who told you?" Eardle wanted to know, looking around the clearing.

"Dusty," the black-dressed Texan answered. "With your lady wives' blessing, I'll have to come right on out and fess up."

"Way you're talking," the boss of the Wedge growled, also glancing around at the men who had made the murderous attempt on the life of him and his companion, "a man'd think there'd been some trouble back to home."

"Nary a trouble that I've seen," the Kid denied. "Which being, Dusty's got things all fixed up to stop any should it come."

"Damn it!" Eardle snapped. "If there's going to be any, I say our place is back there and to hell with seeing the land agent, Stone."

"That's just what your lady said as you'd say, Major," the Kid declared as Kiowa strolled toward where Birt was moaning as he struggled to a sitting position. "And she told us that, should you even *try*, we'd got to rope you both, tie you in your saddles, 'n' haul you to Prescott even should you be kicking 'n' squawling for us not to do same all the way."

"Do you reckon you could do it, Lon?" Stone inquired with a grin.

"I'm not saying's how we could 'n' I'm not saying's how we couldn't," the Kid answered, looking his most baby-faced, his tone almost mild in intonation. "But we'd surely have to give it a whirl. 'Cause, you two maybe-so haven't noticed being married up to 'em, but those are two ladies who are mighty set on getting their way once their minds're made up. Which Kiowa 'n' me don't aim to go back there 'n' say we haven't done their wantings. I'd near on as soon rile up Betty Hardin when she's in one of her do-it-or-else moods."

"Do you know something, Wils?" the boss of the Wedge said to his fellow rancher in a voice heavy with resignation.

"I do, Stone," Eardle declared in a similar fashion. "We're going to Prescott like our ever-loving wives want. There's only one thing for you pair to keep in mind."

"What'd that be, Major?" the Kid inquired.

"If we all get killed while we're there," the boss of the AW ranch said as somberly as if he wanted the two members of the floating outfit to keep every word in mind, "I'm going to have General Hardin *fire* the pair of you."

"Whee-doggie, Major!" the Kid exclaimed. "I should've expected it, the company you're keeping. You're starting to think 'n' talk like a *Texan!*"

146

"Thank God you're here, Captain Fog!" Roger C. Harman gasped, hurriedly coming into the office of the jailhouse shortly after nine o'clock in the morning. "The bank's been *robbed*!"

After a study of the catalogues in Clitheroe's General Emporium had failed to find a weapon capable of handling the kind of bullet that had been fired at Sheriff Amon Reeves, Deputies Rusty Willis and Thorny Bush, acting on the instructions given by the small Texan, had continued the search via a couple of catalogs presented by Mrs. Flora Sutherland from companies dealing directly with the customers through the mail. Although this had also proved abortive, Dusty Fog had decided that the experience would be useful to the youngster in showing him something of the dull and often unproductive routine a peace officer must expect in the execution of his duty.

Despite a thorough search of the area around where the sheriff had been found shot, the lean and buckskin-clad freight-wagon driver, Tumac— who had soon satisfied Dusty that he was competent at his work—fetched by Calamity Jane, had failed to locate any trace of whoever was responsible. He had extended the circumference of the circle in which he made his examination as far as the small Texan estimated the weapon could have been used under the lighting conditions that prevailed at the time of the shooting, but to no avail. Nor had a house-to-house visit made in the general vicinity by Dusty and his deputies found anybody who could say the shot had been heard. Not that the small Texan had expected there would be, although he conceded that it was possible he could be wrong and made the effort as a matter of course. Everybody in the neighborhood had been either a close friend or an admirer of the sheriff, and he felt sure anyone who had heard the shot would have already come to mention the matter.

About an hour after the small Texan and his deputies returned from their efforts, Counselor Edward Sutherland had come to the office and said that the newly arrived lawyer, Nigel Jones, had arranged a satisfactory settlement for the injury caused by the fighting dog to the boy and his pet. In addition, Jones had provided a written statement absolving Dusty and his deputies of any misconduct where the assertions of the men who owned the cantina were concerned, and stating that he hoped the matter would now be considered closed. On being assured by Sutherland, in the capacity of Justice of the Peace for Spanish Grant County—therefore able to speak in behalf of the sheriff and deputies—that it would, the two members of the legal profession had parted with mutual expressions of satisfaction, which were genuine on the part of the local delegate, over the way the affair was resolved. Asked by Dusty what he thought about another member of his profession coming to start up in the town, Sutherland had said he thought it could prove a good thing, as he often found himself caught between the conflicting interests of clients or those he knew as friends who were brought before him in his second capacity. He had then admitted that he wished Jones were a more likable person.

Shortly after Sutherland had left for home,

saying he had considered it advisable to handle the matter in such a fashion, the lawyer had arrived to give Calamity the money that was owed to Dobe Killem for the use of the wagons that provided Derek Hatton and Steven Scott with the means to set them going in their business. Although the receipt of the payment would have allowed the redhead to leave Child City, she had made no mention of doing so. Nor, in the light of something else that took place, had Dusty asked when she intended to take her departure. Watching the arrival at the cantina of half a dozen loudly chattering women who were good-looking in a brassy way and had diverse types of shapely and openly flaunted physiques, he concluded that her services as a deputy capable of dealing with them as members of her own sex might prove useful. However, the need for the redhead to serve in such a capacity had not arisen because the newcomers had remained quietly at what was to be their place of work.

With the cowhands from all four spreads either occupied on the roundup or guarding the respective properties, business had been slow at the Arizona State Saloon and the "house of ill repute" on the edge of the town had also been experiencing a lack of trade when Dusty told Bush to check on it as they were making the rounds. A few of the men who were to be employed at the cantina had been in the former establishment for a short while, causing Dusty to keep his deputies in the vicinity in case of trouble, but nothing untoward had happened and they left peaceably about an hour later.

For the remainder of the time, everything had

continued to be uneventful and, Dusty suspected, boring in Bush's view. In fact, the whole community had given the appearance of having retired for the night shortly after eleven o'clock. Adhering to what Sutherland had said was the routine carried out by Reeves and the now-departed Deputy Burt Alvord, Rusty and Calamity had made a final tour just after midnight. Then, having come to the office to report the pacific conditions that prevailed, the redhead had returned to sleep in her wagon while the small Texan and the other two Texans settled for the unused cots in the cells.

On rising that morning, Dusty had set Rusty and Bush to work sweeping out and generally tidying the jailhouse. Cheerfully asserting that his superior rank gave him the right to do so, Rusty had had Bush do the majority of the work. Far from being annoyed, and showing the kind of spirit that had won him acceptance with the Wedge crew during the cattle drive from Texas, the youngster had sworn he would take revenge when he was sheriff and had one of Rusty's sons as his deputy—then carried out the task with good grace and considerable mock complaining about the unfairness of his being made to do so. Claiming she still had to look after the needs of her team of horses and wagon, Calamity had contrived to arrive just after the work was done. They had breakfasted together in the dining room of the small Summers Hotel farther along the street—and at which they discovered Jones was residing, although they did not see him or want to. They had just returned to the jailhouse, and Dusty was at the point of finding them some work to do, when Harman arrived with his news.

"Scatters!" Rusty snapped to Calamity and Bush, speaking in his capacity as first deputy and remembering the time in Quiet Town when he had helped Dusty deal with an attempt to rob a bank.

"Leave them be, they won't be needed," the small Texan put in briskly before the order could be obeyed. He realized that a robbery of the kind envisaged by the older Wedge hand could not be taking place at that moment or there would have already been some indication of it, and Harman was unlikely to have been let loose to report it if the usual methods in the West were being employed. "When did it happen, Mr. Harman?"

"I don't know *when,* but it *must* have been during the night!" the banker replied in something close to a wail. "I only found out it had happened when I went with Cuth—our guard to open up."

"Do *you* usually do the opening?" Dusty asked, going to collect his Stetson from the set of whitetail deer antlers nailed to the wall by the front door.

"No," Harman answered. "Mr. Canoga is usually there before me, and he does it."

"Uh-huh," Dusty grunted noncommittally.

"But he wasn't there when we arrived," Harman went on. "Which surprised me, as he's generally quite punctual."

"What's gone?" Bush put in before Dusty could pose the same question in a more polite fashion.

"*Everything!*" the banker groaned. "Lord, this is a disaster!"

"*Everything?*" the youngster repeated with a

similar emphasis on the word, drawing a look of disapproval from Harman and also causing a warning glance to be directed his way by Calamity.

"You mean whoever did it took away *every-thing* the bank held?" Dusty queried, giving no indication that he had heard Bush, although he had noticed and agreed with the response from the redhead.

"Well, they left some bonds which wouldn't be negotiable and a few more things they wouldn't be able to dispose of either," Harman elaborated. "But they took *all* the money, and whatever was in the safe-deposit boxes they opened."

"I'll come with you right now," the small Texan stated, donning his hat. "Hold the office down, Rusty."

"Yo!" the older Wedge cowhand responded, the traditional acknowledgment of assent to an order used by the Confederate as well as the Union Cavalry.

"Go fetch Counselor Sutherland, Calam," Dusty went on.

"Is that *necessary*?" Harman asked before the redhead could speak. "If word of what's happened gets out, there will be *panic* all through the town."

"Word will have to get out sooner or later," Dusty declared. "That's why I want the Counselor on hand there as Justice of the Peace for the County. That's the best way to handle things." Then, allowing the banker no opportunity to say anything more, in answer to the unasked question on the face of the youngster, he continued, "You come with me, Thorny!"

152

"Is that wise, Sheriff?" Harman demanded. "He's just a boy—!"

"He's man enough for me to have picked him to wear a badge," the small Texan said coldly. "And I reckon I'm going to need all the help I can get before this business is through."

WHAT ARE YOU *IMPLYING?*

Leaving the sheriff's office before there could be any further conversation, and having told Richard C. Harman to try to act natural since there were a few people around, Dusty Fog contrived to hold the pace to a steady walk as he led the way toward the bank. He was pleased to notice that Thorny Bush was behaving with a passable suggestion of nonchalance. However, the youngster was feeling disappointment over the way things were turning out. When he accepted the offer from the small Texan to be a deputy sheriff, he had thought that dealing with a bank robbery would entail the excitement of going up against a masked gang with roaring guns. Instead, he might have been taking a leisurely stroll on a normal morning.

Acting as if nothing untoward had occurred, Calamity Jane strolled with a deceptive speed in the direction of the Sutherland house. Before coming out onto the street, she had quietly told Bush to allow Dusty to do all the talking and listen and learn how such things should be done. Fortunately, the few men and women on the sidewalk paid scant attention to the agitated way in which the banker was behaving.

On arriving at their destination, Dusty noticed that the Closed sign was still in place on the door. At Harman's knock, access to the building was provided by the young man who acted as bank guard. He was, the small Texan knew, Cuthbert Castle—the banker's brother-in-law, suspected by the local community of having been given the job, because he was not capable of doing anything requiring intelligence or manual dexterity. Certainly nothing about his demeanor struck Dusty as befitting a man whose purpose was to safeguard the bank and its property. Rather, his sallow, unprepossessing features had a guilty look about them, to the small Texan's way of thinking. Dusty wondered whether he felt he had somehow been responsible for the robbery having taken place.

"Don't let *anybody* else in," Harman ordered as he led the way through the door.

"Except Deputy Canary—you'll likely recognize her since she's wearing her badge—and Counselor Sutherland," Dusty supplemented, seeing the lack of comprehension on the guard's face and guessing what had caused it. "She's gone to fetch him, and they'll be wanted inside as soon as they come."

Instead of replying to either speaker, Castle turned his head to look at the woman who stood in the open doorway to the banker's private office.

There was nothing glamorous about Harriet Harman—rather the opposite, in fact—and it was obvious at first glance who was the dominant partner in her marriage. In fact, her brother looked much like a scaled-down and less impressive version of her. Clad in a somber black dress intended to remove as far as possible any trace of womanhood, she was tall and angular. Set in grim lines, her features were gaunt, and her dark eyes held a coldly determined glint.

On meeting Mrs. Harman for the first time while making a check of firearms the previous day, Dusty and Calamity had been received with scant courtesy. Before being in her company for many seconds, having seen no weapons of the kind he was seeking, the small Texan had decided that she reminded him of the kind of woman who sought to compensate for a lack of looks and personality with liberal, feminist ideals of the most virulent variety. Afterward, the redhead had commented that their unwilling hostess had struck her as being tarred by the same brush as a bunch of supposed suffragettes against whom she and the lady outlaw, Belle Starr, had once been in contention.

"Howdy, ma'am," Dusty greeted, removing his hat as he had been taught from early childhood by the female members of the Hardin, Fog, and Blaze clan was the polite thing to do. Having taken a dislike to her, he could not resist turning to her husband as if she were of no importance in the matter. He strolled over to look into the office and noticed only that the door of the vault, which showed no signs of forced entry, was open. There was a closed window, which had a padlock on the inside and stout iron bars outside, and there was no other way of gaining admittance except through the door at which he stood. Nodding as if he had made an important discovery, he directed his gaze past the woman and went on, "I don't see anything to say how they got in."

"Through the front door, of course," Mrs. Harman put in, her manner openly hostile at having been treated in such a fashion. "That's *obvious*. There isn't any other way they could have!"

"That'd take a key, ma'am, way the door looked to me as we came through," the small Texan drawled in the manner of one making an obvious point that had been overlooked by the person he was addressing. "And I don't reckon there'll be too many of them floating about, Mr. Harman."

"Of *course* there aren't!" the woman hissed, giving her husband no chance to speak. "There are only four in existence!"

"Which kind of cuts down on the number of folks who could've done the unlocking, I'd reckon," Dusty asserted, still giving no acknowledgment of the banker's wife. "I conclude you 'n' your broth—guard have one apiece, Mr. Harman, and, going by what you said back to the jailhouse, your man Mr. Canoga must make that three. Who-all has the fourth?"

"I do, of course!" Mrs. Harman snapped.

"And you've all got your keys?" the small Texan asked.

"What are you implying?" the woman demanded with blatant hostility.

"Just wanting to know should any of you just might've happened to have lost your key recent'," Dusty explained, still contriving to give the impression of being a country bumpkin seeking to impress more brainy folks. He sensed his young deputy was both puzzled and distressed by the way he was behaving, but he had no intention of explaining the reason until a more propitious time. "Because, like I said, whoever come in didn't do it by busting down the doors or through the windows."

"Here's *my* key!" Mrs. Harman nearly shouted, taking the key from the black bag she was holding. "Show him yours, Roger, Cuthbert!"

"*Gracias,*" the small Texan thanked when the order was complied with. "That only leaves us with Mr. Canoga. Where's he at?"

"Don't ask us," Mrs. Harman sniffed. "He should have been here by nine o'clock."

"Then I reckon you'd best head for where he lives and bring him back here, Deputy Bush," Dusty ordered.

"Yo!" the youngster answered promptly, relieved to have been given something definite to do and left with a speed that would have made the small Texan smile under different conditions.

"Looks like whoever opened up your vault, or whatever 'n' of those fancy steel boxes is called, used a key," Dusty commented after making a closer examination of the open door of the vault and its contents, ignoring the obvious disapproval being shown by the gaunt woman. "Leastwise, they didn't blow their way in with gunpowder nor dynamite like I've heard tell of happening in other places even out here in the West, 'stead of busting in with masks 'n' drawn guns by day same as Jesse James and Sam Bass do their stickups."

"Why do you keep saying 'they,' " Mrs. Harman challenged.

"Seems to me as how there'd have to be more than just one man, *ma'am,*" Dusty pointed out, emphasizing the last word to give the impression that he objected to being questioned by a woman. He gestured to the open door of the vault and continued, "I'd say there must've been a fair amount of gold 'n' silver coins as well as cash money held in there. More than one man could move, anyways."

"There was," the banker admitted.

"Would you know what was in these boxes?" the small Texan inquired, indicating the open steel containers lying on the floor in front of the vault with a leisurely flick of his left hand.

"Not *everything*," Harman replied. "Their contents are the property of whoever rents them."

"But you know who they belong to?" Dusty suggested.

"Of course," Harman admitted, then continued as if making an explanation to a less than bright child, "However, whatever is put inside is done so by the one who rents each, and we never ask what it might be."

"Major Eardle allowed his lady asked him to put her jewelry in one," Dusty drawled, surprised that he had been allowed to carry on the conversation without Mrs. Harman interrupting.

"Yes," the banker replied. "He did."

"Then they'll be gone," the small Texan said quietly. "Like all the money the Major 'n' Stone Hart depos—left with you."

"The money *everybody* had in the bank has gone," Mrs. Harman put in when her husband hesitated. "Including our own."

Before any more was said, the front door of the bank was thrown open and Calamity came in fast, followed by Sutherland and Bush.

"Dusty!" the redhead snapped, her face showing how grave she regarded the business that had brought her back. "Some kids fooling around a well that isn't used no more back of town've found young Toby Canoga's body in it!"

"Let's go and take a look!" the small Texan snapped with none of the small-town naïveté he had been simulating so well. From the way in which the Harmans and Castle were looking at him, he concluded that they had noticed the change in his attitude, and he got the feeling none of them cared for it. "You folks stay here with Counselor Sutherland and keep the front door locked until I come back. Thorny, go tell Rusty to bring his rope, and you go for Doc Gottlinger, Calam, soon as we're told where-at's the well." After the directions to the well had been supplied by the attorney, he snapped, "Move it, both of you."

"This is another part of being a peace officer, boy," Dusty Fog said gently. Thorny Bush had returned in a shamefaced manner from having gone to vomit behind some nearby bushes. His nausea had been created by the sight of Toby Canoga's body on being retrieved from the well. "And it's close to being the worst part, so there's no shame in it."

"D-don't tell the boys at the Wedge what I've done, *please*," the youngster requested.

"The man who does'll answer for it to *me*!" Calamity Jane asserted grimly. She had had sufficient contact with violent death in her young life to remain apparently unaffected by what she had seen. However, there was anger in her voice as she went on, "Goddamn it, Dusty, what's happening around here?"

"There'll be some who'll reckon he was killed by whoever he was in cahoots with to rob the bank," the small Texan replied.

"*Him?*" the redhead snapped. "Hell, he's just become a poppa and struck me as being a real nice young feller."

"Sam Bass has struck more than one that way," Dusty reminded the irate girl.

"Sam Bass *is* a real nice young feller, by all I've heard," Calamity declared. "You don't reckon that's what come off here, do you?"

"I don't *reckon* anything," the small Texan asserted in a way that told the redhead he wanted the subject closed. Turning to Gottlinger, the tall, bulky medical practitioner for Spanish Grant County, he went on politely, "Can you tell me how and about when he died, Doc?"

"I had experience of such things for the police in the Old Country," Gottlinger replied, making a wry face. "But I thought I had finished with them when I came here. I never *liked* doing it, nor do I think I will now. It's a good thing you have sent everybody but your deputies away. Perhaps you should go, young lady."

"Who's come?" Calamity inquired, gazing about her despite knowing that she was the person to whom the directive had been addressed. The strength of Dusty's personality had caused most of the few people who had gathered to depart; it was she who had persuaded the boys who had found the body to go. She had done this by demonstrating her ability at wielding her long-lashed bullwhip and promising

160

a more lengthy exhibition later. "Go to it, Doc. I've seen my share 'n' more of dead bodies."

"As you will!" Gottlinger grunted, then bent over the corpse to carry out a preliminary investigation. When he was finished, his voice became more Germanic in timbre, as if delivering a report to a law-enforcement officer with whom he had worked in Westphalia before emigrating to the United States. "Death was caused by a thrust into the kidneys from behind with a thin and sharp weapon of some kind and would have been almost instantaneous. It is difficult to be more accurate without an autopsy—!"

"I know what *that* is, Doc," Dusty stated as the words came to a stop and an interrogative glance was directed his way.

"It is difficult to be accurate without an autopsy," Gottlinger resumed. "But I would say he has been dead for several hours, perhaps even since last evening."

"I've heard tell, with an autopsy, you can find out whether a body's been moved after it died, Doc," the small Texan remarked in an almost casual fashion.

"It is possible," Gottlinger admitted. "And, before you ask, Captain Fog, I know how to do so."

"Then I'd be right obliged if you would," the small Texan said quietly, yet in a way that implied he expected a response in the affirmative. "And I reckon it might be useful to be able to nail down when Mr. Canoga died as close as can be."

"That will take some time," the doctor

warned. "By this evening at the earliest, I would say."

"I'd prefer it sooner, if possible," Dusty answered. "Rusty, Thorny, help the Doc get the body to his place. Calam, I want you with me."

"Where're we going?" the redhead inquired.

"To do the dirtiest chore a peace officer ever has to do," the small Texan replied.

Calamity had never known him to speak with such cold sincerity.

AS OFTEN AS HE CAN SNEAK AWAY

"Well, I'll be switched!" announced the woman who was coming along the sidewalk in the business area of Prescott toward the two part-Indian members of General Ole Devil Hardin's floating outfit. They were lounging in an apparently negligent manner on the hitching rail outside a building bearing a large sign on one of its windows announcing in large white letters, LAND AGENT, ARIZONA TERRITORY, J. NICHOLSON. "I heard you was riding scout for Stone Hart's Wedge, Kiowa, and you'd been in some fuss out Backsight way, *Cabrito*. Yet here you are in Prescott, large as life, fit as a flea and close to as lively I hope."

Suggesting that any further conversation be put off until after the wounded survivors of the abortive murder attempt had had their injuries attended to—although he shared Stone Hart's eagerness to learn more about the reason the Ysabel Kid and Kiowa Cotton had been sent away from the work of the roundup—Major Wilson Eardle had said he had acquired enough medical knowledge during his military career to be able to at least stop the bleeding. Wanting to find out what lay behind the thwarted attack, there had been a noticeable reluctance toward this shown by the two Indian-dark Texans. The younger of the pair, no longer giving the slightest impression of his everyday baby-faced innocence, had claimed that it struck him as being a waste of time to give treatment to *hombres* who were not going to make it to Prescott if he and his *amigo* had their way.

The reaction of the Major to what was said had had the effect the Kid had desired. The least affected of the intended killers, also the youngest and most frightened—although neither of the others able to talk showed signs of being much more staunch—John Birt had been eager to try to avert the threatened fate by answering the questions put to him by Stone Hart, while Eardle proved to have enough skill to at least give them a chance to survive the journey to the Territorial capital. However, none of them could say more than that they had been hired by "Taos Lighting"—whose real name none of them claimed to know—to go to Child City and stir up fuss, and failing this, to ambush the two ranchers.

Accepting that all of those questioned were too eager to save their skins and intimidated by the way the Kid and Kiowa hovered in the background, the ranchers had concluded that they had been told the truth. They had also decided what they considered to be the best way to deal with the surviving attackers. Saying that none were in any condition to be moved—although he was sure this was not the case—

Stone had declared that the would-be killers would remain in the clearing until the authorities came to collect them. Believing a refusal might lead the two savage-looking part-Indian Texans to take the reprisals that had been threatened, the would-be bandits had not objected to the proposal. In fact, however, Birt and his cohorts were hoping to escape before the law could arrive.

After learning why Dusty Fog had sent the Kid and Kiowa after them—and admitting that their wives had made good sense in insisting they carry on with what they had come this far to do—the ranchers had stated a desire to get their business in Prescott over as quickly as possible so they could return to their homes in case trouble should be contemplated there. The two members of Ole Devil's floating outfit had taken the precaution of bringing along enough horses for all of them to ride relay and reduce the time required for the journey.

While waiting for the Kid and Kiowa to fetch the animals from where they had been left across the Verde River, the Major stated his admiration for the men's ability to bring the animals along undetected. Stone agreed, but warned with a grin that the praise must never be repeated within earshot of the pair or they were likely to ask for a raise in pay. The boss of the Wedge claimed that such things had been part of the training each man was given in his formative years, and had not been forgotten. He also admitted that, like Eardle, he had come close to believing that they were serious in their intention to kill the captives rather than take them to the authorities.

The party had arrived at Prescott shortly after

noon. After the needs of the leg-weary animals had been seen to, the ranchers and their companions found accommodation at a boarding house and, having tidied up their appearance, set off on the business that had brought them to the territorial capital.

The first thing on the agenda was to notify the authorities of what had happened the previous night. Both ranchers insisted on this, although the Kid and Kiowa claimed it to be a waste of time. They all quickly concluded that—not surprisingly in a Territorial capital—the sheriff of Yavapia County was more adept at riding the political fence than at enforcing the law. Although neither rancher had met Colonel Raines of Backsight, when the Kid suggested that they were on very good terms with him, Sheriff Donald L. Dewar had been all too willing to concede that they had dealt with their attackers in a justifiable fashion under the circumstances. He also promised to have the wounded and dead men fetched to Prescott.

Having dealt with that matter, Stone and Eardle were at liberty to attend to the business that had brought them to the capital. The Kid and Kiowa went along, saying they were taking no chances that the ranchers would sneak back home and get them in hot water with the two feisty ladies who sent them. Sharing Dusty Fog's often-expressed belief that the best way to avoid trouble was to be ready to meet it, Stone and Eardle had raised no objections. However, the two Texans elected to remain on the sidewalk while the conference with the land agent took place.

Though no longer in the first flush of youth,

the speaker who addressed the Kid and Kiowa in such a friendly fashion was certainly good-looking. Although she was dressed in much the same way as the "good" women in the vicinity, some of them went out of their way to avoid going near her. Not that either Texan wondered why this should be. Regardless of the way she dressed and behaved in public, Brenda Wayhill had long been connected with brothels—first as one of the girls and, for some years now, as a madame. That she knew so much about their recent activities came as no surprise to either man, because they knew the speed at which news was passed around the West.

"Howdy, Bren," Kiowa greeted. He and the Kid rose from their places on the hitching rail with an alacrity that drew disapproving glances from some of the females nearby. "I didn't know as how you'd left Kansas."

"Trail driving up there will soon be over, the way railroads are getting pushed every which way into cattle country," the madame explained. As always, her mode of speech suited the person she was addressing. "So I concluded the time had come to light a shuck for pastures new. Was offered a nice house down here in Prescott and thought I might as well give it a whirl, as Arizona's growing richer by the day. Don't tell me that you pair're fixing to take up land because Ole Devil's finally come to his senses and set you afoot like you've always deserved?"

"Nope," the Kid replied, noticing that Brenda Wayhill kept glancing at the window of the Land Office. "Anyways, he allows the OD Connected just wouldn't be the same without us two. Maybe

166

not 'specially better, but not the same. We're just waiting 'round for Stone Hart 'n' Major Eardle to 'tend to their business."

"I hope they get what they've come for," the madame remarked in what seemed a casual fashion.

"But you don't reckon they will," the Kid guessed.

"There's been talk that some other folks're more than a little interested in those two spreads that've been left without owners up to Spanish Grant County," Brenda replied. Both Texans were friends of long standing, to whom she owed a debt of gratitude for a service they had performed for her in the past. "You tell Stone and Wils to ride careful and watch that pious-talking little hypocrite. What I've heard from one of my girls he's real sweet on, he's mixed up in something sneaky that he reckons has already brought him a fair bit of money, and he's looking for more."

"You sound like you don't like that gent in there," the Kid remarked, showing no surprise that Eardle had been referred to by an abbreviation of his given name.

"I liked Wyatt Earp better, if you can believe that, which is why I chose here instead of going down to a pretty good house in Tombstone I was offered," the madame replied. "Nicholson's a lousy hypocrite whose missus runs high in the bunch of bluenoses who're always telling the law to stamp out all houses of ill repute, especially mine where she's concerned. Way she picks on me and mine, you'd reckon she knows her old man's a steady customer."

"Is he, for shame," the Kid drawled. He

167

wondered whether the information could be put to use if the land agent tried to abuse his authority where the two ranchers were involved, although he knew neither rancher would approve of this tactic. "Does said Mr. Nicholson come down often?"

"As often as he can sneak away," Brenda answered. "And he'll be coming tonight for sure. This's the night his missus and her bunch hold one of their meetings, and he always drops by to see Michele around eight o'clock. She's got to calling him her pension fund, he's so all-fired regular. Well, I'd best be on my way before associating with the likes of you pair ruins me socially."

"That'd *hurt*, wasn't it true, Bren," Kiowa sighed. "*Adios*. Don't do nothing we wouldn't mind."

"Which gives me a whole heap of scope, unless doing it would be against nature," the madame declared. "Say 'Howdy, you-all' to Stone and Wils for me, as I don't reckon those two poor gals who've taken them up would want me doing it personally, and especially not in business hours."

"Are you thinking what I'm thinking, *amigo*?" the Kid inquired, glancing at the window of the land agent's office as the woman walked away.

"If you're thinking what I'm thinking you're thinking what I'm thinking," the other Indian-dark Texan answered cryptically. "And I reckon you just could be. Shall I go find where-at Bren's place'd be, Congressman?"

"I yield to the senator from Rio Hondo County, Texas," the Kid declared. "And I'll stay put here just in case them as sent those yahoos've found out what happened and're fixing to make another stab at it."

Although both Texans had continued to keep a watch on their surroundings even while talking with the madame, neither had spotted a man who was keeping them under surreptitious observation.

However, the watcher did not make his presence known at that time. "Why did I *ever* listen to that Steffie Willis?" Matilda Canoga asked pitifully, sitting with her eyes red from crying and her face showing grief as she nursed her baby.

"What about, honey?" Calamity Jane inquired with a gentleness of which people who knew her only slightly would never have believed her capable.

"She said I should make Toby carry on behaving like he always did, now little Toby Junior had come," the newly widowed mother answered.

"And she was *right*!" the redhead claimed definitely, yet kindly. "Had you tied him down, he'd've right soon got to putting the blame on li'l Toby Junior and, was I asked, that's not a good way for a pappy to be with his young 'n'."

"But tonight was the night he went to play poker and have a few beers down at the saloon," Matilda pointed out. "That's why I didn't worry when he wasn't home at his usual time."

After the body had been taken away, and Dusty Fog had given some quiet instructions to Rusty Willis and Thorny Bush, he and she had set off for the home of the dead man. They found that a man had already delivered the news

169

and, fortunately for him, taken his departure before they arrived. Shown in by Mrs. Lucy Wentworth, Canoga's mother-in-law, they had found Matilda in a state of near-incoherent distress. At that moment—not for the first time in their association—the small Texan had found the redhead to be in a situation she had never encountered before. Displaying a sympathy and understanding that he admired and was certain he could not have come even close to duplicating, she had contrived to calm the grieving young woman enough so that the main purpose of the visit could be carried out.

"There was no way you could've knowed tonight was any different from the rest, honey," Calamity pointed out. "Now Cap'n Dusty's going to ask you some questions 'n' see if you can help us get the sons of bit—who did it. And you can bet all you have that we'll not rest until we have."

"Did he often work late down to the bank?" Dusty asked.

"Quite often," Matilda replied. "I always used to think that he was the one who did most of the running of it, the amount that was put on him."

"Was it any special nights he was there?" the small Texan queried. "I mean so that somebody who was fixing to do the robbery would expect him to be on hand?"

"No," the young mother answered, clearly struggling to prevent herself from bursting into tears. "It could be any night when there was work that needed finishing."

"Even if it was his night for poker playing and a few beers with his *amigos* down to the Arizona State?" Dusty continued.

170

"Of course," Matilda asserted. "He is—was—very conscientious."

"More so than those Harmans deserved," Mrs. Wentworth, who had been fond of her son-in-law, put in coldly. She remained in the room at the request of the small Texan.

"Uh-huh!" Dusty grunted. "What did you do when he wasn't home at the usual time?"

"I went to see if he'd got delayed at the saloon," the older woman explained. "Not to chase him up or anything, but I know what fellers are like when one of them's newly become a father. Especially when they're bachelors, which most of them are, they think it's funny to get him to stay out late."

"And when you found he wasn't there and hadn't been?" the small Texan wanted to know. He made no comment on the subject of how young bachelors behaved, though he knew there was some justification for her observation.

"I thought they—the Harmans—could have kept him working at the bank, even though they never had that late. It was dark when I went along, which I didn't think was strange considering the time. As I was looking in the window of Harman's office, I thought I heard a scuffling, but there wasn't nothing to be seen."

"What kind of a scuffling?"

"Oh, just about what mice would make."

"Mice?"

"There are quite a few of them around the bank," Mrs. Wentworth explained. "According to Toby, there's a fair-size cellar underneath. It was put there to be used as a vault, but the feller who had the bank before the Harmans found out that making one down there would be too expensive and decided to put it where it is instead."

"How come the man who had it gave it up?"

"He allowed he was wanting to retire and had had a good offer from the Harmans that would let him do it."

"How long've they been here?"

"About two years. Why?"

"It's best to know as much as you can in cases like this," Dusty said—evasively to Calamity's way of thinking, although neither mother nor daughter appeared to notice. "Maybe whoever did it knew them and their habits afore they got here and figured something from that would help with pulling the robbery. Do you know where they came from?"

"No." Mrs. Wentworth admitted. "They weren't much on sociabilizing. We asked her to join the Child City Civic Betterment League when she first got here, and she said she would but never did."

"Did they make any friends around town?" the small Texan queried, making it sound like idle conversation.

"Not that I know of," Mrs. Wentworth replied. "The only one who I ever saw go visiting at night was that Welsh rancher who was killed, and he didn't call very often."

"Uh-huh!" Dusty grunted. "Well, I'd best be going and seeing what I can learn around town."

"Do you think you'll get whoever kill—did it?" Mrs. Wentworth asked.

"I tell you, ma'am," the small Texan replied, and suddenly there was no pretense in his attitude. Once again he was the dominating figure that the strength of his personality caused him to appear to be in times of stress. "We're going to do *everything* we can to do just that."

"If I get the stupid son of a bitch who must've run all the way here to tell Tildy what happened," Calamity said in throbbing tones of anger as she and the small Texan walked away from the house, "I'm going to make him wish his momma and poppa never met the one time they did."

"That wasn't a nice thing to say, even though I'd be inclined to agree with it," Dusty said. "He likely thought he was acting for the best."

"And so will I!" the redhead promised. She looked at her companion speculatively and went on, "Anyways, what's going on in that tricky li'l Rio Hondo mind of your'n?"

"How do you mean, gal?" the small Texan wanted to know, exuding innocence that was almost convincing.

"All the questions about the Harmans," Calamity elaborated with an air of patience that was likely to disappear at a moment's notice. "And don't feed me no bull droppings about just wanting to know anything that might help. It's the same as with Mark, 'n' 'specially Lon. There's not the one of you a gal can trust when you start looking like butter wouldn't melt in your mouth."

"That's no way for a duly sworn and appointed *deputy* to talk to the sheriff who got her the chore, for shame!" Dusty declared in a pompous-sounding voice.

"Nor'll be me ramming the butt of my bullwhip up his butt end if he can't give a straight answer to a question!" Calamity threatened. "What did you whisper to Rusty 'n'

Thorny so secret-like afore we went our ways?"

"If you *have* to know, ma'am, I said for them to go around to the bank when they'd helped deliver the body to Doc's," Dusty explained with patient resignation. "And they was to stay one front and one back until I told them different."

"Can I ask why you did *that*?" the redhead asked brusquely.

"Could be I reckoned there might be another stab at robbing the bank," the small Texan suggested.

"And Wyatt Earp could be a real nice, up-standing officer of the law, only he sure as shit *ain't*," Calamity snorted. "Anyways, there wouldn't be no point in robbing the bank. There's nothing 'cepting the counselor, the Harmans, him 'n' her, and that weak-kneed brother of her'n left in it."

"I know," Dusty replied. "And I aim to see that it stays that way."

I WANT *EVERYTHING* BACK

"I'm afraid that I have some bad news for you, gentlemen."

Unaware of what was being said on the sidewalk outside his office, John Nicholson was looking distinctly uncomfortable as he faced the two ranchers seated across his desk from him. It was all very well, he thought, for the three men who had demanded his presence at the Spreckley Hotel to give him orders he could not refuse to accept. While they had produced the requisite documentary proof to be used, it

174

was he and not they who had to deliver it and the news, which was not likely to be favorably received.

The land agent had not seen or had contact with any of the trio since the meeting, but he had the uncomfortable feeling that he was being kept under almost constant observation. Therefore, realizing what the consequences would be if he failed to do as he was instructed, he decided he had no alternative than to carry out his order. He took comfort from telling himself that there was no way in which the truth of the matter could be established. Furthermore, at the back of his mind was the thought of the pleasure he would have that evening in the company of somebody he found far more pleasant and consoling than his overbearing and domineering wife.

"In what way?" Major Wilson Eardle inquired in a mild voice.

"I'm afraid both of the properties in which you are interested cannot be offered for sale," the land agent replied.

"Can we ask why not?" Stone Hart drawled, also showing no animosity.

"Their deceased owners left them to kinsmen in wills," Nicholson claimed.

"Do you know this for *sure*?" the Major asked.

"Of course," the land agent asserted, wishing that the ranchers would stop looking at him in so disconcerting a fashion. "It is my place to know, and the necessary documentary proof is in my possession."

"Who are these kinsman?" Stone said gently, showing only mild interest.

"I can't discuss such a confidential matter," Nicholson stated with pompous superiority, for he was now sure he was on safe ground.

"Can we see the proof?" Eardle suggested.

"I'm afraid not, Mist—!" Nicholson began.

"*Major,* if you don't mind!" Eardle interrupted. The barked-out words caused the land agent to make a startled movement.

"I'm sorry, *Major!*" Nicholson said, slumping back against his chair. "But, as I said, the matter is confidential and not one of public record."

"That isn't the way I see it," Eardle said, seeming to grow in stature as the pompous attitude of the land agent deflated. Although he was retired, he was aware of the power the Army possessed in Arizona; as a rule, a Territory had more need than a state for protection against hostile Indians and other foes, and the Army could provide this protection. To press his advantage, he now resorted to a ploy he had once heard used very effectively against a similarly pompous bureaucrat. "You are familiar with Statute Thirty-seven, Article Nineteen, Subsection Twelve, and its subsidiary in the Territorial Charter of Arizona, Article Thirty-six, Paragraph Eleven, Clause Four?"

"Well—!" the land agent began, unwilling to admit his ignorance, particularly of a subject that had been mentioned with such an aura of authenticity.

"Then you must be aware that information of the kind we want to see must be made available to such interested parties who may have cause to wish to do so?"

"I—I—!"

"Who was the attorney your old commanding officer from Hood's Texas Brigade, *Colonel Raines* of Backsight, said we should contact if we had the need of legal assistance, *Captain* Hart?" Eardle asked, pleased that he had remembered the name given by the Ysabel Kid that had produced such fast cooperation from the sheriff of Yavapia County.

"I'll go fetch him, Major," Stone declared, noticing that the reference to his supposed connection with Colonel Raines had not been overlooked by the land agent.

"There is no need to put yourself out in any way, Mist—*Captain* Hart," Nicholson stated hurriedly. Like most bureaucrats, he had learned early in life not to antagonize people who possessed the means to exert influence in high places. "I was merely pointing—!"

"The documentary proof, if you *please*," Eardle said coldly. He had learned early in his career the best way of dealing with a pompous little man like the land agent. "I know you're a busy man, and I don't want to have to take up any more of your time than necessary."

"Or *ours*," Stone growled. "Colonel Raines has asked us to look up a number of his good friends, and it's only common courtesy that we should even if we don't have anything special needing to be talked over."

"I'll get the documents for you!" Nicholson promised. He went to the safe, then returned with the requested documents.

Stone and Eardle examined the documents. Those studied by the boss of the Wedge claimed

177

that the Arrow P had been left by Patrick Hayes to a cousin, Michael Portillo, a resident of Patterson, New Jersey. The others asserted that Eustace Edgar Eisteddfod had bequeathed the Vertical Triple E to a nephew, Evan, of the same surname and an address in Peoria, Illinois. In addition to naming attorneys in the towns who had handled the matter, the wills bore dates showing that they had been drawn up shortly after the owners had taken possession of the properties.

"Well, gentlemen?" Nicholson said, having watched the ranchers pore over and exchange the documents. "Are you *satisfied*?"

"They look like they'll hold water," Stone admitted in a grudging fashion.

"There's nothing wrong with them that I can *say*," Eardle conceded, sounding no better pleased. "I can't see any point in taking up more of Mr. Nicholson's valuable time, Captain Hart, can you?"

"No," the boss of the Wedge answered, wondering whether the land agent had noticed the slight emphasis Eardle had placed on the word "say." "It looks like we'll just have to make do with the land we've got, Major Eardle."

The ranchers rose and left the office seemingly in angry frustration, and Nicholson let out a long sigh of relief. Then he took out his handkerchief to mop the perspiration on his face and neck. He hoped the sweat and his anxiety had gone unnoticed. Telling himself he would never again become involved in such a piece of blatant chicanery, he returned the documents to the safe. When its door was locked and the key pocketed, he returned to his desk and slumped down on his chair to recover his badly shaken equilibrium. More than ever, he was looking forward to making love with Michele that evening.

The land agent would not have been so complacent if he had been able to overhear the conversation taking place outside his office.

"How'd it go, gents?" the Kid inquired as the ranchers emerged and he joined them on the sidewalk.

"Bust," Stone replied. "Seems both Eisteddfod and Hayes left their spreads to kin back east."

"Met Bren Wayhill while you was talking in there," the black-dressed Texan remarked in a casual fashion that did not fool either of his companions. "Not that either of *you'd* know her, being respectable married men 'n' scared of your wives. She allowed as how you wouldn't be let have the spreads."

"Did Bren say why?" Eardle asked.

"Not in so many words," the Kid admitted. "Only, I've allus found she was pretty close to right in everything she said 'n' did. There's no chance of something sneaky about them kin who are getting the spreads?"

"The documents *look* legal enough," the Major admitted. "Except I would swear they'd all been produced by the same set of hands."

"I thought you'd noticed that," Stone claimed. "Trouble being, they're so damned well done only an expert could say whether we're right or wrong."

"Pinkerton's have some experts along those

lines," Eardle said pensively. "The trouble being, getting them to have one come out here
will take time—and money."

"I'll cut it evens with you," Stone said. "Let's
go see their local office, if there is one."

"There's sure to be, this being the capital and
so much general lawbreaking going on all
through the Territory," the Major assessed. "All
we have to do is ask around and go there when
we're told where it is. Are you still going to
dog us like our ever-loving wives told you, Lon?"

" 'Til night, anyways," the Kid answered.
"Unless you're going to be roaming around after
dark."

"After the way we came here, I'm for a good
night's sleep," Eardle declared.

"And me," Stone supported. "Would you and
Kiowa have the same notion, Lon?"

"Nope," the black-dressed Texan answered.
The hectic journey to Prescott after the abortive attack had caused him to be somewhat less
vigilant than would normally have been the case,
and he had failed to detect the man who was
keeping them under observation. "After we've
grabbed us the smidgin of rest all us Injuns
need, we've got it in mind to go visit Bren and
get acquainted with a li'l gal called Michele,
should she be free."

"I *demand* to know why we have been kept here
so long, sheriff!" Harriet Harman snarled as
Dusty Fog came through the front door of the
bank on Calamity Jane's heels.

"As I have told you before, Mrs. Harman,"
Counselor Edward Sutherland injected,
employing his most impressive official de-

meanor, before the small Texan could speak. "Captain Fog and I felt it advisable for you to remain on the premises so you could explain why the bank was closed, without creating the kind of panic your husband is so keen to avoid, and rightly so."

It was close to sundown, and the lamps had needed to be lit in the building. In their glow, the woman, her husband, and her brother were showing signs of strain.

The attorney had been able to deflect various inquiries as to why the bank was not open for business, but he felt it was only a matter of time before somebody connected this with Toby Canoga's death. Fortunately, some of his best and most reliable friends had been among the earliest arrivals, and he was able to enlist their support in preventing the true state of affairs from being made public.

After the interview with Matilda Canoga and Mrs. Wentworth, Dusty had kept Calamity and himself occupied, awaiting whatever Doctor Klaus Gottlinger might have to report. Fetched by the redhead, Tumac had been asked to try to find tracks, but the area had not been conducive to this type of search. All the freight-wagon driver had been able to say with any certainty was that the body had been carried to and dropped into the well. He could not discern any suggestion of who had done the deed, and could be no more specific as to what time it occurred beyond saying that it appeared to be before dawn.

Like Sutherland at the bank, the small Texan was attempting to prevent what had happened from becoming public knowledge. In all the time

181

the redhead had known him, she had never been more impressed by the way he dealt with a situation. He employed diplomacy and, when this seemed unavailing, adopted such a chilling demeanor that—with one exception—the matter was simply dropped. The exception, one of the men brought to Child City to work at the *cantina,* had been dealt with by Dusty in a swift and painful fashion.

A short while earlier, Calamity had been keeping her promise to the two youngsters who had found the body by giving them an exhibition of her skill with her long bullwhip. However, a message from the doctor instructing her to join the small Texan had caused her to bring the display to an end. The expression on Dusty's face told her that something important was about to take place.

"You've had one of your men out front and another at the back," the woman accused, looking at Dusty and giving no indication of having heard what the attorney had said. "Why was that?"

"You could say it was to stop anybody sneaking around and finding out for sure what's happened," the small Texan explained. "Anyways, I'm here now, and there's only one thing I want to say."

"And what is that?" Mrs. Harman asked, staring at the dusty-blond Texan and wondering how she had ever mistaken him for a simple rube.

"I want everything back!" Dusty said quietly, yet with a grim and deadly force.

"I *beg* your pardon?" Mrs. Harman snapped, her right hand slipping into the large handbag, which she had not permitted to leave her sight all the while she was prevented from leaving the bank.

"Don't!" Dusty commanded. He paid no attention to either Roger Harman or Cuthbert Castle, although their faces registered a mixture of alarm and guilt. "I want everything you took from the vault brought out of the cellar where you put it while those two were taking Toby Canoga's body to dump it down the well after you'd killed him."

"Damn you!" Harman screamed, lunging toward his wife. "You said they said there'd be a man—!"

The words were brought to an abrupt end by the crash of a shot from a heavy-caliber handgun.

Flame spurted from the side of the bag in the woman's hands. Even as her husband was reeling back, blood coming from a wound in his right breast, she brought into view the Merwin & Hulbert Army Pocket revolver that she had produced for inspection when Dusty and Calamity paid the visit to her home. She clearly intended to keep firing, and she clearly possessed the ability to shoot effectively, as she already had when shooting at her husband.

Dusty drew his matched Colt Civilian Model Peacemakers with the speed for which he had acquired fame through the West, then hesitated as he aimed them and cocked the hammers with his thumbs. All was ready for the guns to be fired, but this did not happen. Despite knowing he was up against a cold-blooded and ruthless person, he could not compel himself to send bullets into a woman.

It was fortunate for the small Texan and

Sutherland that Calamity did not share his scruples. Although Dusty had not mentioned his suspicions, his attitude had warned her that trouble of a serious nature could be forthcoming, and she had guessed whence it would come. Therefore, she had taken action upon seeing the scowling gaunt woman slip her hand into the bag. Unnoticed by anybody, she had turned her right hand palm out to close around the ivory handle of her holstered Navy Colt.

Although unable to match Dusty's speed on the draw, the redhead had brought out her weapon in time to play a central role in the quickly unfolding drama. The first bullet she cut loose took its intended target just below the right breast. However, although Mrs. Harman was jolted on her heels by the impact, she neither dropped her revolver nor showed any indication of losing her resolve to kill Dusty.

Calamity reacted as any trained gunfighter would under the same conditions. Quickly elevating the Colt to shoulder height at arm's length in both hands, she sighted and shot again. This time the .36-caliber conical piece of lead passed between the woman's eyes and through her brain to burst out at the rear of her skull. Mrs. Harman was killed instantly as she pitched over backwards, but not before she sent another round from her weapon that narrowly missed the small Texan's head and ended its flight in the wall.

"*Gracias*, Calam!" Dusty breathed, returning his Colts to their holsters. He realized he had had as narrow an escape from death as at any other time in his life.

"The pleasure was all mine," the redhead

answered, also replacing her weapon. There was no levity in her voice. "I reckon Tildy and her li'l 'n' deserved it, what that bitch did to Toby."

"You won't get any argument from me on that," the small Texan claimed. "Go tell Rusty to send Thorny for the Doc. I want Harman able to do some talking, and fast."

Even before Gottlinger arrived, the banker and his equally terrified brother-in-law had given all the information they possessed. Neither knew who had been behind Mrs. Harman's gaining control of the bank and arranging for it to be robbed. However, Harman explained that she had carried out the shooting of Sheriff Amon Reeves with a rifle that she had not produced for inspection and that was now hidden in the cellar—the entrance to which was beneath his desk—with the knife from the handle of her parasol and the contents of the vault. With the local peace officer out of the way, a replacement was to have been provided who would ensure that the blame was placed on the dead teller, whose body should not have been found. The replacement had not arrived, but Mrs. Harman had insisted that the scheme she had worked out proceed as planned. To throw suspicion Canoga's way, she had murdered him with the knife from the parasol as he was getting ready to leave for the day, and had his body removed in the early hours of the morning.

What Dusty heard had confirmed the suspicions he had already formed. He had realized that the contents of the vault could not have been removed from the building without assistance and some means of transport. Although this could have been done after he and his deputies had turned in for the night, his every instinct had suggested this was not the case. Mrs. Wentworth's revelation about the cellar had merely corroborated his belief that such a place existed. The autopsy carried out by Gottlinger had established that the killing took place in the early evening, and the corpse's post mortem lividity proved it had been moved some time after death occurred.

With all this information at his disposal, the small Texan had arrived at the bank ready to try to provoke a response by letting it be known he was aware of the truth. He had also guessed it would be the banker or guard who broke down, but the deadly response of the woman when the former had done so took him by surprise. Fortunately, Calamity had had the quickness of wits to save him from what could easily have proved a fatal error.

"I reckon you've heard all you need, Counselor," Dusty said after the two men had finished talking. "There's one thing, though. I reckon a reward's coming for getting the loot back. Can I count on you to see that Matilda and her li'l 'n' gets it to make up for what they've lost?"

"You *can*!" the attorney stated.

WAS I YOU, I'D *TALK*

Despite having received an unexpected visit from Graeme Steel just before closing his office for the day, John Nicholson was in a more relaxed frame of mind than at any other time since the discussion with the two ranchers earlier in the day. It had been obvious that the conspirator, with whom he had had the most dealings, knew that Stone Hart and Major Wilson Eardle had called. Informed of what had taken place, Graeme had shown no concern over discovering that the interested parties from Spanish Grant County had seen the documents purporting that there were still owners of the Arrow P and Vertical Triple E ranches. This was understandable, although the land agent did not know why. It was Graeme who had produced the forgeries, and he was delighted that they had evidently been accepted as bona fide by the two ranchers. He had been so gratified by the news that he had presented Nicholson with a bonus of a hundred dollars—although he would later claim the sum to be two hundred and fifty when demanding recompense from Willis Norman and Anthony Blair.

Nicholson was of course unaware of what developed elsewhere after the visits, especially with respect to the activities of the ranchers, who had already put the matter of the suspect documents in the hands of the Pinkerton National Detective Agency's local office. He had had the good fortune to find his wife even less interested than usual in how he was planning to spend his evening: listening to a Jesuit priest famous in her circle for his outspoken opposition to pleasures enjoyed by the masses in general and houses of ill repute in particular. As usual, she had accepted without question that he had work that prevented him from accompanying her, and went without him. His own infidelity notwithstanding, he would have been furious if he had known that she herself was having an affair with the Catholic clergyman whose sermon they attended every Sunday.

Left to his own devices, the land agent could hardly restrain his ardor until it was dark enough for him to set off for a clandestine visit to the discreetly located house run by Mrs. Brenda Wayhill. As he hurried through the deserted area of town beyond which his destination lay, his thoughts were devoted solely to the pleasures he was anticipating. He did not doubt that these would be increased after he presented to Michele seventy-five of the dollars given to him by Steel as a bonus. Even if he had been more alert to his surroundings, he would not have been able to avoid what was coming so suddenly and unexpectedly did it happen.

With alarm, Nicholson sensed two dark shapes converge on him from around the corner of the last building before the open space in front of the small copse on the route to his destination. What followed numbed him into such terror that he was unable to even think of how to respond, much less take any kind of positive action.

A hand grasped the back of the loose, detachable celluloid collar worn by the land agent.

At the same instant, he felt a sharp instrument being pressed against his lower garments to prick gently into his spine.

To add to his terror, he heard a voice chilling in its savage intensity.

"Don't make no fuss, Mr. Land Agent, else you won't be able to go see that li'l gal of your'n ever no more!"

The warning delivered, the captors began to guide Nicholson away from his intended destination toward the edge of the town.

On being joined by Kiowa Cotton, who had obtained instructions for locating the house operated by Brenda Wayhill, the Ysabel Kid had decided on what he believed was the best way to handle the situation that had arisen as a result of the visit to the office of the land agent. However, he had kept it to himself until he and his even more Indian-dark and dangerous-looking *amigos* were waiting nearby for their charges to visit the local representatives of the Pinkerton National Detective Agency. Giving what had seemed like grudging acceptance of the example of Pehnane Comanche Dog Soldier ingenuity he received, Kiowa had conceded he could think of no better or potentially enjoyable way for them to achieve the desired results.

When assured that neither Stone Hart nor Major Wilson Eardle intended to leave the boardinghouse where they had obtained accommodation, the pair had set off to make preparations for putting the plan into effect. Going to the small area of woodland just outside the limits of Prescott that they had noticed in passing while riding in along the stagecoach trail, they had been fortunate enough to find all except one thing they required to achieve their purpose. Not only was there a clearing of sufficient size for their needs, but a big white oak had been felled and cut into logs of dimensions that rendered it unnecessary for them to search for anything else. These had been carried and placed beneath the spreading branches of a sturdy cottonwood.

Having gathered enough dried leaves and small pieces of wood for their purpose, the two Texans had made their way to Brenda Wayhill's place of business. They were greeted at the back door, which was not usually available for access by visitors. William, her large, jovial and very loyal Negro cook, had asked no questions when told what they wanted. Nor, remembering the debt that she owed them, had Brenda proved any more inquisitive on learning what they wanted, and she was able to supply them with what they needed from the kitchen instead of having to send William in search of it. Taking to the clearing, the three-foot-square thin iron used as a warming plate for food, they had set it in position over the two logs and placed the other material they had gathered underneath. Then they had gone in search of their prey. Not that locating the land agent had posed any problems. All they had needed to do was lurk in concealment near the brothel and wait for him to keep his regular rendezvous with Michele. They had agreed to compensate the girl for the loss of her night's earnings with a little bit of extra cash for her pension fund if they achieved the results they hoped for.

The two men, so well-versed in the art of silent movement and keeping captives responsive to their wishes, had achieved the first part of their plan without difficulty.

Nor, feeling the lack of active response from the land agent, did the Kid and Kiowa anticipate that the rest of their plot would produce any greater problems. John Nicholson was on the point of collapse, and his legs felt as if they were turning to water beneath him. If he should collapse, he felt certain that his captors might use to lethal effect the sharp knife he could still feel through his now sweat-sodden underclothing. But despite his terror, the last thing he intended to do was yell for help. Not only was the area through which he was being hustled outside the limits of Prescott, making it most unlikely that there would be anybody close enough to hear, but he did not doubt that he would be silenced permanently and in a painful fashion before assistance could be rendered. His throat was so dry that he could not even ask why he was being treated in such fashion.

Arriving in the clearing with the shivering and unresisting man, who was staring about him with a total lack of comprehension, the Ysabel Kid and Kiowa Cotton wasted no time in making him ready for what they planned to do. While the former kept the bowie knife in position, the latter took off Nicholson's derby hat and celluloid collar with its clip-on necktie. Then, handled with the deftness acquired through dealing with recalcitrant horses, he was just as quickly subjected to having his Hersome gaiter boots and socks removed. Then, much to his growing consternation, his wrists were secured behind his back by a leather pigging thong and he was compelled by a gentle prick from the knife to step onto the iron plate lying across two logs.

"Wh—What are you going to do?" Nicholson managed to croak as he stood swaying on the cold, level surface.

"Now, I'd say as how that depends on *you*,"

Kiowa answered and for the first time the land agent realized that both he and his companion had their bandannas drawn up as masks to prevent them from being identified at a later date. "You know something we want to know, and we conclude you're going to tell us all about it."

"Don't *hurt* me!" Nicholson wailed, but he was so terrified he did not dare move.

"Nope, we're not going to hurt you one li'l bit," the Kid asserted, but his voice lacked conviction. He was deftly dropping the loop of the rope around the land agent's neck and flipping its stem over a stout limb of the cottonwood tree that extended above the structure upon which he had been compelled to stand. "Now, would li'l ole us, Kiowa?"

"We wouldn't hurt a fly," the other Indian-dark Texan affirmed with seeming sincerity. "Not 'less'n it wouldn't tell us what we want to know."

"Y-y-you daren't hang me!" Nicholson stated, but his voice—never authoritative unless dealing with somebody over whom he felt it was safe to flaunt his position of power, which certainly was not the case at such a moment—was totally lacking in conviction.

"Who-all's fixing to *hang* you?" the Kid inquired mildly, although the man he was addressing did not consider him in any way gentle. "Why, doing that'd be plumb ag'in the legal law."

"It surely would," Kiowa agreed. " 'Course, we can't do nothing to stop *you* should you get to feeling like hanging yourself."

"M-myself!" the land agent repeated. "W-why should I do *that?*"

"Maybe 'cause that ole metal plate you're

standing on started getting too hot for you to bear it no more," the Kid offered as he knotted the unused end of the rope in what looked to be a secure fashion to the trunk of the tree.

"I-it's not *that* hot," Nicholson stated, and stared in horror at what he saw being done by the older of his masked captors.

"Nope, it ain't—*yet*," Kiowa drawled, applying the match he had lit with a flick of his left thumb to the dry material in the space left beneath the plate. "But I'd surely hate to put my money down on it staying that way."

"Nor me," the Kid claimed. "Was I you, I'd *talk*. No matter how much you got paid for what you did about those two spreads in Spanish Grant County, you won't be able to spend a thin dime of it after the sheriff says, 'Well what do you know, he's *dead!*'"

"I d-don't know what you mean!" the land agent stated in a wavering tone.

"Could be having your feet warm up more'n a mite'll make you change your mind," Kiowa hinted, watching the fire he had started begin to grow in intensity so its flames licked at the bottom of the iron sheet.

"Ever seed a man die hanging, *amigo*?" the Kid inquired. "I mean *slow*, not like when a regular legal-appointed hanging-man does it on a proper set up gallows."

"Can't say I have," the other Texan admitted, giving the impression that he was ashamed to be compelled to make the confession.

"I have, just the one time," the Kid asserted, with what sounded to Nicholson like satisfaction. "It was surely real *slow* in doing, 'n' looked tolerable painful." He paused to let the gist of

193

the comment sink in, then continued, "So what've you got to tell us about them documents for the ranches you showed Cap'n Hart 'n' Major Eardle, *hombre*?"

"Like how come they was supposed to come from two towns no place anywhere near close together, but both'd been writ in the same fist," Kiowa continued, and thrust some more of the gathered kindling onto the flames.

"I—I was told they were *genuine!*" Nicholson claimed, wishing he had the courage to start screaming at the top of his voice.

"Who told you?" the Kid asked.

"I d-don't kn—!" the land agent began.

"Stoke her up a smidgen more, *amigo*," the younger Texan requested.

"I don't know their names!" Nicholson croaked, hoping his legs would continue to support him. He was just as conscious of the coarse feel of the running noose about his neck as the metal plate, which was growing closer to a heat he would be unable to bear. "Honest to God, I *don't!*"

"Looks like he's just natural' going to have to hang hisself, *amigo*," Kiowa stated, pushing some more fuel into the gap between the logs.

"I don't know all their names!" the now panic-stricken land agent insisted. "But there are three of them involved, and I was told I had to meet them at the Spreckley Hotel."

"Where they told you they was sending along fake documents saying as how there was fellers who owned the two spreads?" the Kid suggested.

"I—I wasn't told they'd be forgeries!" Nicholson babbled, moving his feet in an attempt to lessen the effect of the growing heat. "Steel just sai—!"

The words were brought to a stop by the sound of a revolver shot from the woods at the edge of the clearing.

Struck in the head, Nicholson was pitched backward from the plate.

Even as the land agent was falling and the knot with which the rope had been held in place performed its intended function by allowing it to slide away from the trunk, the two Texans flung themselves away from the faint glow of the fire. Going to the ground with his right hand starting to bring the old Colt Dragoon revolver from its low cavalry twist-hand-draw holster, only the extreme rapidity with which he moved saved the Kid from becoming a victim to the next shot fired from the darkness of the trees. He had felt the wind of the lead passing just above his head as he plunged for safety.

Instead of moving clear of the land agent, Kiowa plunged with an equal alacrity so as to keep partially shielded behind his body. Nor did the precautionary measure he had taken prove unnecessary. Coming with what might have been considered commendable speed and accuracy, the third bullet passed through the space just vacated by his body. He, too, held his revolver by the time he alighted on the ground.

"You see him, Lon?" Kiowa breathed, hugging the ground and scanning the area from which the shooting had taken place.

"Nary a sight nor sound," the Kid admitted after a moment, and in no louder a tone. "I tell you, *amigo,* whoever the son of a bitch is, he can sure move real quiet to get there without us hearing anything of him coming."

"That's for certain *sure,*" Kiowa conceded in grudging admiration. "And he can shoot better'n fair too."

WE'VE NO WAY WE CAN PROVE ANYTHING AGAINST THEM

"Time we figured it was safe to get up and take after him, way he could handle his gun," the Ysabel Kid told Stone Hart and Major Wilson Eardle as they sat in Hart's room with Kiowa Cotton listening by the door to prevent the conversation being overheard by chance or deliberate intent. "The son of a bitch was up and gone without a goddamned sound to say which way he'd lit a shuck."

"He should never've got up so close without one of us hearing him," the second Indian-dark Texan asserted bitterly. "Don't you go along with me on that, Lon?"

"I do!" the Kid declared in a similar fashion.

"Goddamn it, after the day you'd had, it's only natural you wouldn't be at your best," Eardle pointed out. He knew the emotions being shown by the pair were not simulated as a means of obtaining exculpation for having committed an avoidable error. "I don't know about Stone, but I was close to asleep on my feet when we left the Pinkertons. We came here to grab some rest, but you pair had a hell of a lot of work to do before you could get any."

196

"You're right enough on that, Wils," the boss of the Wedge ranch confirmed. "Hell, you two did everything humanly possible to even bring off as much as you did."

"So Nicholson told you the three men he met were at the Spreckley Hotel, did he?" the Major asked, wondering whether the Indian-dark duo would have gone through with the hanging if they had failed to receive the answers they were demanding.

"That's what he said, which I reckon he was scared too close to white-haired to lie," the Kid replied. "We'd've gone down to say, 'Howdy, you-all' to 'em straight off, but reckoned we'd best fix things so that real smart sheriff of Yavapia County wouldn't guess what had been happening and maybe come to figuring out the truth."

"How did you do that?" Stone inquired, having noticed the far-from-flattering reference to the senior local peace officer and concurring with the sentiments that caused it.

"After we was sure that light-moving 'n' gun-handy *hombre* really had lit a shuck 'n' wouldn't be coming back, we got Nicholson dressed proper ag'in," the Kid explained. "We did all we could to clear up what we'd been at by making it look as if the fire'd been set by a couple of hunters and toted off the iron plate to hide it where it's not likely to be found for a fair spell unless it's being looked for special, which we don't figure is like' to happen, kind of lawmen they've got hereabouts, even should they get 'round to doing the looking. Then we toted him, making like we was helping to fetch home a feller who had drunk more'n enough, down towards the edge of town; but no place near

Bren's, her being a real good friend and right helpful through all this. Emptied his pockets like he'd been killed for what he was carrying and headed out. We'll pass on the money to that li'l gal he was headed to meet, 'cause we caused her to lose what she calls her pension fund. Anyways, with that done, we concluded we'd best come and let you know what'd come off so you could decide what to do next."

"There's no point in going to the Spreckley," Eardle claimed after a few seconds of thought. Giving vent to a grunt of annoyance, he went on, "Even if they are still there, we've no way we can prove anything against them."

"Should you be able to get them, even just one, like you did Nicholson it wouldn't help," Stone drawled, eyeing his fellow Texans in a speculative and, knowing them very well, prohibitive fashion.

"It'd warm their tiny li'l feet more'n a mite," the Kid pointed out. "Which I reckon they'd likely talk like he did."

"Sure," the boss of the Wedge conceded. "Only, the kind of law-wranglers they'd hire have them get up in court and allow they was made to and only did it to save themselves from what was being done. Which wouldn't help our chances of proving that the documents about ranches aren't the real thing."

"So what do we do?" Kiowa growled.

"Get a good night's sleep, all of us," Eardle stated. "Then, comes morning, we'll go around to the Spreckley and find out what kind of men we're up against."

"We know's one of 'em's damned good at

sneaking around 'n' shooting," the Kid declared with feeling. "Don't we, Kiowa?"

"If he ain't," the other member of Ole Devil's floating outfit supplemented, "He'll do me right fine 'til somebody who's *good* comes 'round."

"He's likely only a hired man," Stone surmised. "A damned good one, I'll grant you, but I'm willing to bet he's just a li'l Indian and not one of the chiefs. It's the men at the top and what they're figuring on doing that we want to find out about."

"And then?" the Kid asked.

"We'll have to figure out how to stop them," Stone declared, and the Major nodded in grim concurrence.

"AND that's how it was, gents," Jack Straw stated, looking from one to another of the three conspirators in the room at the Spreckley Hotel where he had first met them.

He had made his way to the establishment after having silenced John Nicholson, and the hired gun had just finished describing the result of his having been successful in keeping the Ysabel Kid and Kiowa under undetected observation. Not wanting to let the trio feel he was belittling his own activities, as doing so could reduce the faith in him that he felt would prove more profitable than was so far the case, he refrained from mentioning that he attributed his achievements against two such competent adversaries solely to both of them being at lower than their usual standard of capability. They had reached Prescott soon after having brought to an end the attempt made upon the lives of the two ranchers by the men led by Michael

Round, so they had to be tired. He had required all his skill in the art of silent movement—under poor lighting conditions—to merely make the approach to the clearing through the woodland without betraying his presence to the normally keen-eared and very alert part-Indian Texans. Nor had getting off the three shots been any mean feat, even though only one had had the required effect. He was equally grateful for having been able to make his escape without being followed.

Taken all in all, Straw decided that he had done a very excellent day's work.

"How much had that bastard told them?" Willis Norman demanded in his usual surly New Englander tones.

"I dunno," Straw admitted, but without the slightest suggestion of apology for having to make the negative response. "Hell's fires, you don't go rushing up promiscuous when you're up against them two half-breed sons of bitches. I had to ease through the piny woods so slow 'n' careful they'd've had time to get him spilling his guts about everything he'd done since he was the sneaky, sniveling kid I'm certain sure he used to be."

"Then you didn't hear *anything*?" Anthony Blair asked in as nearly an indignant fashion as he dared employ.

"Sure I did," Straw corrected, deriving satisfaction from knowing what was coming next. "He told as how you three was staying here at the Spreckley."

"He did *what*?" Graeme Steel yelped in alarm, and his associates registered a similar state of consternation.

"That's just what he did," Straw confirmed dryly. "I heard him with my own li'l shell-like ears while I was drawing bead on him to stop him telling anything more. Then, just as I was satisfied I got a right true bead to kill him stone dead instant like, he let out your name, Mr. Steel."

"Goddamn it!" the small and undistinguished-looking man snarled, his face losing all its color. "What are we going to *do?*"

"*Run!*" Straw instructed, his manner implying that he had said all that was required on the subject.

How the three conspirators reacted to the danger is told in ARIZONA GUN LAW.

Appendix One

Following his enrollment in the Army of the Confederate States,[1] by the time he reached the age of seventeen, Dustine Edward Marsden "Dusty" Fog had won promotion in the field to the rank of captain and was put in command of Company "C," Texas Light Cavalry.[2] At the head of them throughout the campaign in Arkansas he had earned the reputation for being an exceptional military raider and worthy contemporary of Turner Ashby and John Singleton "the Gray Ghost" Mosby, the South's other leading exponents of what would later become known as "commando" raids.[3] In addition to averting a scheme by a Union general to employ a virulent version of what was to be given the name "mustard gas" following its use by Germans in World War I[4] and preventing a pair of pro-Northern fanatics from starting an Indian uprising that would have decimated much of Texas,[5] he had supported Belle "the Rebel Spy" Boyd on two of her most dangerous assignments.[6]

At the conclusion of the War Between the States, Dusty became the *segundo* of the great OD Connected ranch its brand being a letter *O* to which was attached a *D* in Rio Hondo County, Texas. Its owner and his maternal uncle, General Jackson Baines "Ole Devil" Hardin, CSA, had been crippled in a riding accident and was confined to a wheelchair.[7] This placed much responsibility, including the need to handle an important mission with the future relationship between the United States and Mexico at stake upon his young shoulders.[8] While carrying out the assignment, he met Mark Counter and the Ysabel Kid, *q.v.* Not only did they do much to bring it to successful conclusion, they became his closest friends and leading lights of the ranch's floating outfit.[9] After helping to gather horses to replenish the ranch's depleted *remuda*,[10] he was sent to assist Colonel Charles Goodnight[11] on the trail drive to Fort Sumner, New Mexico, which did much to help Texas recover from the impoverished conditions left by the War.[12] With that achieved, he had been equally successful in helping Goodnight convince other ranchers that it would be possible to drive large herds of longhorn cattle to the railroad in Kansas.[13]

Having proved himself to be a first-class cowhand, Dusty went on to become acknowledged as a very competent trail boss,[14] roundup captain,[15] and town-taming lawman.[16] Competing in the first Cochise County Fair in Arizona, against a number of well-known exponents of very rapid drawing and accurate shooting with revolvers, he won the title "The Fastest Gun in the West."[17] In later years, following his marriage to Lady Winifred Amelia "Freddie Woods" Besgrove-Woodstole,[18] he became a noted diplomat.

Dusty never found his lack of stature an impediment to achievement. In fact, he occasionally found that it helped him to achieve a purpose.[19] To supplement his natural strength,[20] also perhaps with a desire to distract attention from his small size, he had taught himself to be completely ambidextrous.[21] Possessing perfectly attuned reflexes, he could draw either, or both, his Colts whether the 1860 Army Model[22] or their improved "descendant," the fabled 1873 Model "Peacemaker"[23] with lightning speed and shoot most accurately. Furthermore, Ole Devil Hardin's "valet," Tommy Okasi, was Japanese and a trained *samurai* warrior.[24] From him, as was the case with the General's "granddaughter," Elizabeth "Betty" Hardin,[25] Dusty learned jujitsu and karate. Neither form of unarmed combat had received the publicity they would be given in later years and were little known in the Western Hemisphere at that time. Therefore. Dusty found the knowledge useful when he had to fight with bare hands against larger, heavier, stronger men.

1. Details of some of Dustine Edward Marsden "Dusty" Fog's activities prior to his enrollment are given in Part Five, "A Time for Improvisation, Mr. Blaze," J.T.'S HUNDREDTH.

2. Told in YOU'RE IN COMMAND NOW, MR. FOG.

3. Told in THE BIG GUN, UNDER THE STARS AND BARS, *Part One, "The Futility of War,"* THE FASTEST GUN IN TEXAS, *and* KILL DUSTY FOG!

4. Told in A MATTER OF HONOUR.

5. Told in THE DEVIL GUN.

6. Told in THE COLT AND THE SABRE *and* THE REBEL SPY.

6a. More details of the career of Belle "the Rebel Spy" Boyd can be found in MISSISSIPPI RAIDER; BLOODY BORDER; RENEGADE THE HOODED RIDERS; THE BAD BUNCH; SET A-FOOT; TO ARMS! TO ARMS! IN DIXIE!; THE SOUTH WILL RISE AGAIN; THE QUEST FOR BOWIE'S BLADE;

Part Eight, "Affair Of Honour," J.T.'S HUNDREDTH, and Part Five, "The Butcher's Fiery End," J.T.'S LADIES.

7. Told in Part Three, "The Paint," THE FASTEST GUN IN TEXAS.

7a. Further information about the General's earlier career is given in the Ole Devil Hardin and Civil War series. His death is recorded in DOC LEROY, M.D.

8. Told in THE YSABEL KID.

9. "Floating outfit": a group of four to six cowhands employed by a large ranch to work the more distant sections of the property. Taking food in a chuck wagon, or "greasy sack" on the back of a mule, they would be away from the ranch house for long periods and so were selected for their honesty, loyalty, reliability, and capability in all aspects of their work. Because of General Hardin's prominence in the affairs of Texas, the OD Connected's floating outfit were frequently sent to assist such of his friends who found themselves in difficulties or endangered.

10. Told in .44 CALIBRE MAN and A HORSE CALLED MOGOLLON.

11. Rancher and master cattleman Charles Goodnight never served in the Army. The rank was honorary and granted by his fellow Texans out of respect for his abilities as a fighting man and leader.

11a. In addition to playing an active part in the events recorded in the books referred to in Footnotes 13 and 14, Colonel Goodnight makes "guest" appearances in Part One, "The Half Breed," THE HALF BREED, its "expansion," WHITE INDIANS, and IS-A-MAN.

11b. Although Dusty Fog never received higher official rank than Captain, in the later years of his life he, too, was given the honorific "Colonel" for possessing the same qualities.

12. Told in GOODNIGHT'S DREAM Bantam Books, USA, July 1974 edition retitled THE FLOATING

OUTFIT, *despite our already having had a volume of that name published by Corgi Books, UK, see Footnote 9 and* FROM HIDE AND HORN.

13. *Told in* SET TEXAS BACK ON HER FEET *although Berkley Books, New York, retitled it for their October 1978 edition* VIRIDIAN'S TRAIL, t*hey reverted to the original title when reissuing the book in July 1980 and* THE HIDE AND TALLOW MEN.

14. *Told in* TRAIL BOSS.

15. *Told in* THE MAN FROM TEXAS.

16. *Told in* QUIET TOWN; THE MAKING OF A LAWMAN, THE TROUBLE BUSTERS, DECISION FOR DUSTY FOG, CARDS AND COLTS, THE CODE OF DUSTY FOG, THE GENTLE GIANT, THE SMALL TEXAN, *and* THE TOWN TAMERS.

17. *Told in* GUN WIZARD.

18. *Lady Winifred Besgrove-Woodstole appears as "Freddie Woods" in* THE TROUBLE BUSTERS; THE MAKING OF A LAWMAN; THE GENTLE GIANT; BUFFALO ARE COMING!; THE FORTUNE HUNTERS; WHITE STALLION, RED MARE; THE WHIP AND THE WAR LANCE; *and Part Five, "The Butcher's Fiery End,"* J.T.'S LADIES. *She also "guest stars" under her married name, Mrs. Freddie Fog, in* NO FINGER ON THE TRIGGER *and* CURE THE TEXAS FEVER.

19. *Three occasions when Dusty Fog utilized his small size to his advantage are described in* KILL DUSTY FOG!; *Part One, "Dusty Fog and the Schoolteacher,"* THE HARD RIDERS; *its "expansion,"* TRIGGER MASTER; *and Part One, "The Phantom of Gallup Creek,"* THE FLOATING OUTFIT.

20. *Two examples of how Dusty Fog exploited his exceptional physical strength are given in* TRIGGER MASTER *and* THE PEACEMAKERS.

21. *The ambidextrous prowess was in part hereditary. It*

was possessed and exploited with equal success by Freddie and Dusty's grandson, Alvin Dustine "Cap" Fog, who also inherited his grandfather's Hercules-in-miniature physique. Alvin utilized these traits to help him become acknowledged as one of the finest combat pistol shots in the United States during the Prohibition era and to earn his nickname becoming the youngest man ever to hold rank of Captain in the Texas Rangers. See the Alvin Dustine "Cap" Fog series for further details of his career.

22. Although the military sometimes claimed derisively that it was easier to kill a sailor than a soldier, the weight factor of the respective weapons had caused the United States Navy to adopt a .36-caliber revolver, while the Army employed the larger .44. The reason was that the weapon would be carried on a seaman's belt and not handguns having been originally and primarily developed for use by cavalry on the person or saddle of a man who would be doing most of his traveling and fighting from the back of a horse. Therefore, the .44 became known as the "Army" calibre, and the .36, the "Navy."

23. Details about the Colt Model of 1873, more commonly known as the "Peacemaker," can be found in those volumes following THE PEACEMAKERS *on our list of titles in chronological sequence for the Floating Outfit Series.*

24. "Tommy Okasi" is an Americanized corruption of the name given by the man in question, who had left Japan for reasons that the Hardin, Fog, and Blaze families refuse to divulge even at this late date, when he was rescued from a derelict vessel in the China Sea by a ship under the command of General Hardin's father.

25. The same members of the Hardin, Fog, and Blaze families cannot or will not make any statement on the exact relationship between Elizabeth "Betty" and her "grandfather," General Hardin.

25a. Betty Hardin appears in Part Five, "A Time for

Improvisation, Mr. Blaze," J.T.'S LADIES; KILL DUSTY FOG!; THE BAD BUNCH; McGRAW'S INHERITANCE; TRIGGER MASTER; *Part Two, "The Quartet,"* THE HALF BREED; *its "expansion,"* TEXAS KIDNAPPERS; THE RIO HONDO WAR, *and* GUNSMOKE THUNDER.

Appendix Two

With his exceptional good looks and magnificent physical development,[1] Mark Counter presented the kind of appearance many people expected of a man with the reputation gained by his *amigo*, Captain Dustine Edward Marsden "Dusty" Fog. It was a fact of which they took advantage when the need arose.[2] On one occasion, it was also the cause of the blond giant being subjected to a murder attempt, although the Rio Hondo gun wizard was the intended victim.[3]

While serving as a lieutenant under the command of General Bushrod Sheldon in the War Between the States, Mark's merits as an efficient and courageous officer had been overshadowed by his unconventional taste in uniforms. Always something of a dandy, coming from a wealthy family had allowed him to indulge in his whims. Despite considerable opposition and disapproval from hide-bound senior officers, his adoption of a "skirtless" tunic in particular had come to be much copied by the other rich young bloods of the Confederate States Army.[4] Similarly in later years, having received an independent income through the will of a maiden aunt, his taste in attire had dictated what the well-dressed cowhand from Texas would wear to be in fashion.

When peace had come between the North and the South, Mark had accompanied Sheldon to fight for Emperor Maximilian in Mexico. There he had met Dusty Fog and the Ysabel Kid. On returning with them to Texas, he had received an offer to join the floating outfit of the OD Connected ranch. Knowing that his two older brothers could help his father, Big Ranse, to run the family's R Over C ranch in the Big Ben country and considering life would be more enjoyable and exciting in the company of his two *amigos* he accepted.

An expert cowhand, Mark had become known as Dusty's right bower. He had also gained acclaim by virtue of his enormous strength. Among other feats, it was told how he used a treetrunk in the style of a Scottish caber to dislodge outlaws from a cabin in which they had forted up,[5] and broke the neck of a Texas longhorn steer with his bare hands. He had acquired further fame for his ability at bare-handed roughhouse brawling. However, due to spending so much time in the company of the Rio Hondo gun wizard, his full potential as a gunfighter received little attention. Nevertheless, men who were competent to judge such matters stated that he was second only to the small Texan when it came to drawing fast and shooting accurately with a brace of long-barreled Colt revolvers.

Many women found Mark irresistible, including Martha "Calamity Jane" Canary.[6] However, in his younger days, only one the lady outlaw Belle Starr held his heart.[7] It was not until several years after her death that he courted and married Dawn Sutherland, whom he had first met on the trail drive taken by Colonel Charles Goodnight to Fort Sumner, New Mexico.[8] The discovery of oil on their ranch brought an added wealth to them, and this commodity now produces the major part of the income of the present members of the family.[9]

Recent biographical details we have received from the current head of the family, Andrew Mark "Big Andy" Counter, establish that Mark was descended on his mother's side from Sir Reginald Front de Boeuf, notorious as the lord of Torquilstone Castle in medieval England[10] and lived up to the family motto, "Cave Adsum."[11] However, the blond giant had not inherited the very unsavory character and behavior of his ancestor, although a maternal aunt and her son, Jessica and Trudeau Front de Boeuf, behaved in a way that suggested they had done so.[12]

1. Two of Mark Counter's grandsons, Andrew Mark "Big Andy" Counter and Ranse Smith, inherited his good looks and exceptional physique, as did two great-grandsons, Deputy Sheriff Bradford "Brad" Counter and James Allenvale "Bunduki" Gunn. Unfortunately, while willing to supply information about other members of his family, past and present, "Big Andy" has so far declined to allow publication of any of his own adventures.

1a. Some details of Ranse Smith's career as a peace officer during the Prohibition era are recorded in THE JUSTICE OF COMPANY "Z," THE RETURN OF RAPIDO CLINT AND MR. J.G. REEDER, *and* RAPIDO CLINT STRIKES BACK.

1b. Brad Counter's activities are described in Part Eleven, "Preventive Law Enforcement," J.T.'S HUNDREDTH, and the Rockabye County series, covering aspects of law enforcement in present-day Texas.

1c. Some of James Gunn's life story is told in Part Twelve, "The Mchawi's Powers," J.T.'S HUNDREDTH, and the Bunduki series. His nickname arose from the Swahili word for a handheld firearm of any kind, bunduki, and gave rise to the horrible pun that when he was a child he was "Toto ya Bunduki," meaning "son of a gun."

2. One occasion is recorded in THE SOUTH WILL RISE AGAIN.

3. The incident is described in BEGUINAGE.

4. The Manual of Dress Regulations for the Confederate States Army stipulated that the tunic should have "a skirt extending half way between hip and knee."

5. The legacy also caused two attempts to be made on Mark's life. See CUT ONE, THEY ALL BLEED and Part Two, "We Hang Horse Thieves High," J.T.'S HUNDREDTH.

6. "Right bower": second in command, derived from the name given to the second-highest trump card in the game of euchre.

7. Told in RANGELAND HERCULES.

8. Told in THE MAN FROM TEXAS, this is a rather "pin the tail on the donkey" title used by our first publishers to replace our own, ROUNDUP CAPTAIN, which we considered far more apt.

9. Evidence of Mark Counter's competence as a gunfighter and his standing compared to Dusty Fog is given in GUN WIZARD.

10. Martha "Calamity Jane" Canary's meetings with Mark Counter are described in Part One, "The Bounty on Belle Starr's Scalp," TROUBLED RANGE; its "expansion," CALAMITY, MARK AND BELLE; Part One, "Better Than Calamity," THE WILDCATS; its "expansion," CUT ONE, THEY ALL BLEED; THE BAD BUNCH; THE FORTUNE HUNTERS; THE BIG

HUNT; *and* GUNS IN THE NIGHT.

10a. Further details about the career of Martha Jane Canary are given in the Calamity Jane series; also Part Seven, "Deadwood, August the 2nd, 1876," J.T.'S HUNDREDTH; *Part Six, "Mrs. Wild Bill,"* J.T.'S LADIES; *and Part Four, "Draw Poker's Such a Simple Game,"* J.T.'S LADIES RIDE AGAIN, *in which she "costars" with Belle Starr, q.v. She makes a "guest" appearance in Part Two, "A Wife for Dusty Fog,"* THE SMALL TEXAN.

11. How Mark Counter's romance with Belle Starr commenced, progressed, and ended is told in Part One, "The Bounty on Belle Starr's Scalp," TROUBLED RANGE; *its "expansion,"* TEXAS TRIO; THE BAD BUNCH; RANGELAND HERCULES; THE CODE OF DUSTY FOG; *Part Two, "We Hang Horse Thieves High,"* J.T.'S HUNDREDTH; THE GENTLE GIANT; *Part Four, "A Lady Known as Belle,"* THE HARD RIDERS; *its "expansion,"* JESSE JAMES'S LOOT; *and* GUNS IN THE NIGHT.

11a. Belle Starr "stars" no pun intended in CARDS AND COLTS; *Part Four, "Draw Poker's Such a Simple Game,"* J.T.'S LADIES RIDE AGAIN; *and* WANTED! BELLE STARR.

11b. Belle also makes "guest" appearances in THE QUEST FOR BOWIE'S BLADE; *Part One, "The Set-Up,"* SAGEBRUSH SLEUTH; *its "expansion,"* WACO'S BADGE; *and Part Six, "Mrs. Wild Bill,"* J.T.'S LADIES.

11c. We are frequently asked why it is that the "Belle Starr" we describe is so different from a photograph that appears in various books. The researches of the world's foremost fictionist genealogist, Philip Jose Farmer author of, among numerous other works, TARZAN ALIVE, A Definitive Biography of Lord Greystoke *and* DOC SAVAGE, His Apocalyptic Life *with whom we consulted have established that the lady about whom we are writing is not the same person as another, equally famous, bearer of the name. However, the present-day members of the Counter family who supply us with information have asked Mr. Farmer and ourselves to keep her true identity a secret, and this we intend to do.*

12. Told in GOODNIGHT'S DREAM *and* FROM HIDE AND HORN.

13. This is established by inference in Case Three, "The Deadly Ghost," YOU'RE A TEXAS RANGER, ALVIN FOG.

14. See IVANHOE, *by Sir Walter Scott.*

15. "Cave Adsum": roughly translated from Latin as "Beware, I Am Here."

16. Information about Jessica and Trudeau Front de Boeuf can be found in CUT ONE, THEY ALL BLEED; *Part Three, "Responsiblity to Kinfolks,"* OLE DEVIL'S HANDS AND FEET; *and Part Four, "The Penalty of False Arrest,"* MARK COUNTER'S KIN.

Appendix Three

Raven Head, only daughter of Chief Long Walker, war leader of the Pehnane Wasp, Quick Stinger, Raider Comanche's Dog Soldier lodge and his French Creole *pairaivo*,[1] married an Irish-Kentuckian adventurer, Big Sam Ysabel, but died giving birth to their first child.

Baptized "Loncey Dalton Ysabel," the boy was raised after the fashion of the Nemenuh.[2] With his father away from the camp for much of the time, engaged upon the family's combined businesses of mustanging catching and breaking of wild horses[3] and smuggling, his education had largely been left in the hands of his maternal grandfather.[4] From Long Walker, he learned all those things a Comanche warrior must know: how to ride the wildest freshly caught mustang, or make a trained animal subservient to his will while "raiding", a polite name for the favorite pastime of the male Nemenuh, stealing horses; to follow the faintest tracks and just as effectively conceal signs of his own passing[5]; to locate hidden enemies, or keep out of sight himself when the need arose; to move in silence on the darkest of nights, or through the thickest cover; to know the ways of wild creatures[6] and, in some cases, imitate their calls so well that others of their kind were fooled.[7]

The boy proved a most excellent pupil at all the subjects. Nor were practical means of protecting himself forgotten. Not only did he learn to use all the traditional weapons of the Comanche,[8] when he had come into the possession of firearms, he had inherited his father's Kentuckian skill at shooting with a rifle and, while not real fast on the draw taking slightly over a second to bring his Colt Second Model of 1848 Dragoon revolver up and fire, whereas a tophand could practically halve that time he could perform passably with it. Furthermore, he won his Nemenuh "man-name," Cuchilo, Spanish for "Knife," by his exceptional ability at wielding one. In fact, it was claimed by those best qualified to judge that he could equal the alleged designer in performing with the massive and special type of blade that bore the name of Colonel James Bowie.[9]

Joining his father in smuggling expeditions along the Rio Grande, the boy became known to the Mexicans of the border country as *Cabrito* the Spanish name for a young goat a nickname that arose out of hearing white men refer to him as the "Ysabel Kid," but it was spoken very respectfully in that context. Smuggling was not an occupation to attract the meek and mild of manner, yet even the roughest and toughest of the bloody border's denizens came to acknowledge that it did not pay to rile up Big Sam Ysabel's son. The education received by the Kid had not been calculated to develop any overinflated belief in the sanctity of human life. When crossed he dealt with the situation like a Pehnane Dog Soldier to which war lodge of savage and most efficient warriors he had earned initiation swiftly and in an effectively deadly manner.

During the War Between the States, the Kid and his father had commenced by riding as scouts for Colonel John Singleton "the Gray Ghost" Mosby. Soon, however, their specialized knowledge and talents were diverted to having them collect and deliver to the Confederate States authorities in Texas supplies that had been purchased in Mexico, or run through the blockade by the United States Navy into Matamoros. It was hard and dangerous work,[10] but never more so than the two occasions when they became engaged in assignments with Belle "the Rebel Spy" Boyd.[11]

Soon after the War ended, Sam Ysabel was murdered. While hunting down the killers, the Kid met Captain Dustine Edward Marsden "Dusty" Fog and Mark Counter. When the mission upon which they were engaged was brought to its successful conclusion, learning the Kid no longer wished to go on either smuggling or mustanging, the small Texan offered him employment at the OD Connected ranch. It had been in the capacity as scout rather than ordinary cowhand that he was required, and his talents in that field were frequently of the greatest use as a member of the floating outfit.

The acceptance of the job by the Kid was of the greatest benefit all around. Dusty acquired another loyal friend who was ready to stick with him through any kind of peril. The ranch obtained the services of an extremely capable and efficient fighting man. For his part, the Kid was turned from a life of petty crime with the ever-present danger of having his illicit activities develop into serious law-breaking and became a useful and law-abiding member of society. Peace officers and honest citizens might have found cause to feel grateful for that. His Nemenuh upbringing would have made him a terrible and murderous outlaw if he had been driven into a life of violent crime.

Obtaining his first repeating rifle a Winchester Model of 1866, although known at that time as the "New Improved Henry," nicknamed the "Old Yellowboy" because of its brass frame while in Mexico with Dusty and Mark, the Kid had soon become an expert in its use. At the First Cochise County Fair in Arizona, despite circumstances compelling him to use a weapon with which he was not familiar,[12] he won the first prize in the rifle-shooting competition against stiff opposition. The prize was one of the legendary Winchester Model of 1873 rifles that qualified for the honored designation "One of a Thousand."[13]

It was, in part, through the efforts of the Kid that the majority of the Comanche bands agreed to go on the reservation, following attempts to ruin the signing of the treaty.[14] It was to a large extent due to his efforts that the outlaw town of Hell was located and destroyed.[15] Aided by Annie "Is-A-Man" Singing Bear a girl of mixed parentage who gained the distinction of becoming accepted as a Nemenuh warrior[16] he played a major part in preventing the attempted theft of Morton Lewis's ranch from provoking trouble with the Kweharehnuh Comanche.[17] To help a young man out of difficulties caused by a gang of card cheats, he teamed up with the lady outlaw, Belle Starr.[18] When he accompanied Martha "Calamity Jane," Canary to inspect a ranch she had inherited, they became involved in as dangerous a situation as either had ever faced.[19]

Remaining at the OD Connected ranch until he, Dusty, and Mark met their deaths while on a hunting trip to Kenya shortly after the turn of the century, his descendants continued to be associated with the Hardin, Fog, and Blaze clan and the Counter family.[20]

1: Pairaivo: *first, or favorite, wife. As is the case with the other Comanche terms, this is a phonetic spelling.*

2: Nemenuh: *"the People," the Comanches' name for themselves and their nation. Members of other tribes with whom they came into contact called them, frequently with good cause, the "Tshaoh," the "Enemy People."*

3. A description of the way in which mustangers operated is given in .44 CALIBRE MAN *and* A HORSE CALLED MOGOLLON.

4. Told in COMANCHE.

5. An example of how the Ysabel Kid could conceal his tracks is given in Part One, "The Half Breed," THE HALF BREED *and its "expansion,"* WHITE INDIANS.

6. *Two examples of how the Ysabel Kid's knowledge of wild animals was turned to good use are given in* OLD MOCCASINS ON THE TRAIL *and* BUFFALO ARE COMING!

7. *An example of how well the Ysabel Kid could impersonate the call of a wild animal is recorded in Part Three, "A Wolf's a Knowing Critter,"* J.T.'S HUNDREDTH.

8. *One occasion when the Ysabel Kid employed his skill with traditional Comanche weapons is described in* RIO GUNS.

9. *Some researchers claim that the actual designer of the knife that became permanently attached to Colonel James Bowie's name was his oldest brother, Rezin Pleasant. Although it is generally conceded that the maker was James Black, a master cutler in Arkansas, some authorities state it was manufactured by Jesse Cliffe, a white blacksmith employed by the Bowie family on their plantation in Rapides Parish, Louisiana.*

9a. *What happened to James Bowie's knife after his death in the final assault of the siege of the Alamo Mission, San Antonio de Bexar, Texas, on March 6, 1836, is told in* GET URREA *and* THE QUEST FOR BOWIE'S BLADE.

9b. *Since all of James Black's knives were custom made, there were variations in their dimensions. The specimen owned by the Ysabel Kid had a blade eleven and a half inches in length, two and a half inches wide, and a quarter of an inch thick at the guard. According to William "Bo" Randall, of Randall-Made Knives, Orlando, Florida a master cutler and authority on the subject in his own right James Bowie's knife weighed forty-three ounces, having a blade eleven inches long, two and a quarter inches wide, and three-eighths of an inch thick. His company's Model 12 "Smithsonian" Bowie knife one of which is owned by James Allenvale "Bunduki" Gunn, q.v., details of whose career can be found in the Bunduki series is modeled on it.*

*9c. One thing all "bowie" knives have in common, re-
gardless of dimensions, is a "clip" point. The otherwise
unsharpened "back" of the blade joins and becomes an
extension of the main cutting surface in a concave arc,
whereas a "spear" point which is less utilitarian is formed
by the two sides coming together in symmetrical curves.*

*10. An occasion when Big Sam Ysabel went on a mis-
sion without his son is recorded in* THE DEVIL GUN.

11. Told in BLOODY BORDER *and* RENEGADE.

12. The circumstances are described in GUN WIZARD.

*13. When manufacturing the extremely popular Win-
chester Model of 1873 rifle which they claimed to be the
"Gun Which Won the West" the makers selected all those
barrels found to shoot with exceptional accuracy to be fitted
with set triggers and given a special fine finish. Originally, these were inscribed "1 of 1,000," but this was later
changed to script: "One of a Thousand." However, the title
was a considerable understatement. Only 136 out of a
total production of 720,610 qualified for the distinction.
Those of a grade lower were to be designated "One of a
Hundred," but only seven were so named. The practice
commenced in 1875 and was discontinued three years later
because the management decided it was not good sales
policy to suggest that different grades of gun were being
produced.*

14. Told in SIDEWINDER.

15. Told in HELL IN THE PALO DURO *and* GO
BACK TO HELL.

*16. How Annie Singing Bear acquired the distinction
of becoming a warrior and won her "man-name" is told
in* IS-A-MAN.

17. Told in WHITE INDIANS.

18. Told in Part Two, "The Poison and the Cure,"
WANTED! BELLE STARR.

19. Told in WHITE STALLION, RED MARE.

20. Mark Scrapton, a grandson of the Ysabel Kid, served

*as a member of Company "Z," Texas Rangers, with Alvin
Dustine "Cap" Fog and Ranse Smith respectively, grandson
of Captain Dustine Edward Marsden "Dusty" Fog and
Mark Counter during the Prohibition era. Information
about their specialized duties is recorded in the Alvin Dustine
"Cap" Fog series.*

If you have enjoyed reading this large print book and you would like more information on how to order a Wheeler Large Print book, please write to:

Wheeler Publishing, Inc.

P.O. Box 531
Accord, MA 02018-0531

Purchased for
the Sauk Centre
Library
by the
Fraternal
Order
of
Eagles Auxiliary